FROZEN HEART, MELTING KISS

FROZEN HEART, MELTING KISS

BY

ELLIE DARKINS

MILLS & BOON

First published in Great Britain 2014
by Mills & Boon, an imprint of Harlequin (UK) Limited,
Large Print edition 2015
Eton House, 18-24 Paradise Road,
Richmond, Surrey, TW9 1SR

© 2014 Ellie Darkins

ISBN: 978-0-263-25592-8

Harlequin (UK) Limited's policy is to use papers that are natural, renewable and recyclable products and made from wood grown in sustainable forests. The logging and manufacturing processes conform to the legal environmental regulations of the country of origin.

Printed and bound in Great Britain
by CPI Antony Rowe, Chippenham, Wiltshire

For Betty

CHAPTER ONE

'YOU ARE GOING to try this one.'

Maya Hartney forced the corners of her mouth up into a professional smile while she waited for Will Thomas to bite. Behind her back she clasped her hands to stop herself chewing at a nail.

She'd tried dozens of combinations of dishes for this tasting, even though squeezing in an extra job next month was pushing her business to its limits. But it had been impossible to say no when Rachel, Will's assistant, had pleaded with her so earnestly to consider catering for an Appleby and Associates gala dinner.

These moments, waiting for a client to try one of her dishes, were nerve-racking but necessary. Once they'd taken a bite her nerves gave way to sheer pleasure. She loved to watch people enjoy her food. Ever since the first time it had happened, years ago, when she'd first cooked for her university housemates, it had given her a physical thrill.

The joy that her food brought showed in the small smile people gave as they closed their eyes and savoured the taste for a moment. Now, ten years later, she lived and worked for that moment.

And she'd never had reason to doubt her food's capacity for bringing joy. Until now.

Will Thomas had already refused to try her starter, and her flutter of nerves congealed into a lump of dejection as she realised he probably wouldn't try this course either.

Maya swallowed awkwardly, thinking hard, wondering where she had gone wrong. Her late night last night had seemed worth it, if it meant she had this dish just right, but there must be something that she'd misjudged. She bit her lip for a second as she ran through the possibilities in her mind and her pulse picked up speed as she considered improvements she could make. Maybe the dressing *was* a little too acidic? But then he hadn't even tried it, so he wouldn't know that. It must be the presentation that needed more work. The rest of the meal would have to be perfect to get this pitch back on track.

It had nothing to do with the fact that her mouth had watered the first second she'd seen Will

Thomas and he'd met her gaze with steel-grey eyes. It was because she'd felt the chill of his presence since the second he'd arrived, and her whole body had wanted her to resist it. To fill the room with light and colour so that the cold couldn't take hold of her. She'd fought too hard against it to let it in now.

There wasn't a splash of colour anywhere in the office: grey walls, grey carpet, glass table and black leather chairs. She'd not experienced a chill like this for ten years, and would be a happy woman if she never felt it again. There was colour in every part of her life these days, displacing cold grey memories; now this room threatened to undo a decade's positive thinking.

When Will Thomas had walked in the room had suddenly made perfect sense. Charcoal suit, crisp white shirt, black hair with just a few flecks of silver at the temples. Grey eyes that bore an expression as clinical as their surroundings. Despite all this attraction had prickled at her skin, along with a warning, and she'd had to take a breath to steady herself.

His gaze had left his smartphone only briefly, dropped from her face to trace the contours of her curves and finally she'd seen a brief spark of heat in his eyes. The light had been there for just a fraction of a second before he'd caught it, extinguished it, and taken a step away from her, his eyes snapping back to his phone.

She'd crossed her ankles to stop herself taking a step forward, sensing that he wanted space, trying to respect that. Her eyes, though, had seemed desperate to pursue Will Thomas, to roam over the lines and planes of his face, down to where his shirt, crisp and starched and white, was open at the collar.

She'd introduced her starter: a salad of hand-harvested scallops, pan-fried and served with rocket and prosciutto, finished with a dressing it had taken two full evenings to perfect. He'd given it a derisive look and asked her to move on, his fingers twitching on the screen of his phone. Email withdrawal, she assumed. She'd catered for enough business dinners to recognise the symptoms. But the knowledge that he was choosing to check his emails over trying her food made her restless. Her food always spoke for her—what was she meant to do with someone who refused to listen?

On this man those chiselled cheekbones and intriguing silver eyes were entirely resistible.

She closed her mouth and bit the inside of her cheek to stop herself from a very unprofessional outburst.

He *had* to try this dish. She was certain that it would fix their impasse. If he would just give the food a chance *she* could still win him over. She'd sourced tender duck from a nearby farm and selected only the most beautiful vegetables from her local supplier. The herbs had come from the garden of her cottage in the Cotswolds and the sauce, a delicate balance of wine, red berries and orange, was—as of last night's final run-though—perfect.

She wanted it to be right, needed it to be perfect, because if she could no longer rely on her food what else did she have to offer?

Taking a step towards him, she brandished the fork.

'You *are* going to try this one,' she repeated with renewed determination.

She tried to paste the smile onto her face again to soften the blow, but there was no disguising the fact that this was an instruction, not a request, and her frustration had made her words short and sharp.

Will met her gaze and seemed to study her; his eyes narrowed while he inspected her features, as if weighing up his opponent. He slipped the smartphone into his pocket and took the fork from her.

'Do I have a choice?'

Maya couldn't be certain but a ghost of a smile had seemed to flicker at the corner of his mouth. His eyes left her face only briefly as he forked a mouthful of the meat and dipped it into the sauce. She grew warm under his relentless scrutiny and thought again of that moment when she'd first seen him. His eyes had widened when he'd noticed her standing in the conference room, as if he couldn't quite take her in, as if he didn't understand her. She didn't want to be difficult to understand. She had no interest in being enigmatic. What she needed was for him to like this dish, to restore her belief in her food—in herself.

For a moment as he chewed she thought she'd done it, that her food had broken this man's icy resolve. He closed his eyes for a moment, and she was sure he was savouring the flavours she'd worked so hard to blend and perfect. His body stilled, his breathing was slow, his fingers were at rest on his phone. The muscles of his face hinted at a smile. But then in an instant it was gone; his eyes snapped open and she saw only indifference.

'That's fine.'

Fine? *Fine?* Perhaps she'd imagined it, she thought. That moment when it had seemed, however briefly, that he had been won round. Or maybe she hadn't, and he was just determined for some reason *not* to enjoy her food, whatever she put in front of him. Anger at his uninterest prickled—how could he be so determined not to enjoy something she had poured her joy and happiness into?

This wasn't going to get any better, she realised then. She just had to find a way to get through this. To protect herself from the barbs of his coldness until she could get out of there. She relaxed her hold on her anger, bringing it to the fore, letting it protect her from his cold indifference.

'Dessert?' she asked, dreading the response, dreading the rejection, but wanting to get it over with.

'I'm sure you've got that under control.'

'Blackberry fool?' Why not show him how his

dismissal hurt? she thought. It wasn't as if he would even care or notice. And it might make her feel a little better.

His eyes held hers and she felt the heat in her face sink to her belly when he continued to stare at her. She shifted under his scrutiny, trying not to wonder what he was thinking, why he was studying her irises. It seemed that her anger could reach him where her food hadn't.

Will raised an eyebrow. 'It sounds like you've got the measure of things, Miss…'

'Maya's fine,' she said, her words still terse.

'Maya,' he repeated, his voice a little less steady than it had been.

He took a deep breath and she saw a blank mask descend over his face, shutting out whatever it was that had flashed between them in the past few seconds. It was a pattern, she realised. A few seconds when his features flickered with emotion, some pleasure or enjoyment. And then he chased it away, locked his face down hard. His voice too, when he spoke next, was the model of professionalism, his words hard and steady.

'Thank you for coming, Maya. Leave your quote with my assistant and someone will be in touch.'

Anger fought for room with sorrow and the pain that had haunted her since her childhood. Will had shut her out in a fraction of a second. It had taken him the space of a blink to forget whatever it was that had made him pause and consider her the moment before. And she couldn't help but remember how her parents had so easily done the same.

He'd reduced everything that she'd created to a string of numbers on a spreadsheet. A simple calculation that took no account of love and passion. She couldn't meet his eye—didn't know if he was even trying to as she shook his hand. As he walked out she let her frustration loose as she tossed cutlery and crockery back into bags and boxes and then packed away the barely touched food.

She tried rationalising what had happened to make herself feel a little better. It wasn't that he wasn't interested in her food, it was just that he only cared about the numbers. Perhaps she should have guessed the moment he'd walked into the room that this was just another business meeting for him.

She'd never been so infuriated by anyone in her life, she thought as she headed out to her car. It wasn't just his lack of enthusiasm for her food, it was the way that he'd seemed completely unwilling to let himself enjoy it, his determination to see life in columns and cells. He'd only tried one course out of three: her food had never stood a chance of impressing him because he had never been prepared to let it.

That thought drained her anger, sapped the tension from her muscles, as she remembered the last time her passion been faced with pure indifference.

Even if she was offered the job she knew she wouldn't be seeing him again. She knew that to cook, and cook well, for that man after today's disaster would be impossible—a complete waste of good food and time, and too close to too many bad memories. She couldn't do it.

Will glanced at his watch and then back over his shoulder as he waited for Maya to come to the door. He shouldn't be here. He'd tried to convince Rachel to do it for him, but she had told him that going against Sir Cuthbert Appleby was more than her job was worth, that he'd have to suck it up and do it himself. So he'd spent his evening crawling through Cotswold villages—time away from the office that he really couldn't afford—in order to ask for something he desperately didn't want.

He looked up at the front of the cottage as he waited and cringed. Just like Maya, the house was a riot of colour. Roses crept up the warm sandstone, over the door and up towards the thatch, and window boxes overflowed with bright-coloured flowers.

When she'd walked out of his office two days ago he'd thought—hoped—that he would never have to see her again. Even the thought of it had made his skin prickle. There was something about her that disturbed him, something that he couldn't ignore no matter how much he might want to. In those moments when he'd dared to look her straight in the eye he'd seen her every emotion flash across her face. She'd worn her love for her food openly and extravagantly. He'd flinched away from it, intimidated in the face of such an out-pouring of emotion, fearful of its effect on his iron self-control.

If he'd had any other choice he'd have stayed as far away from Maya Hartney as he could. What did he care who they hired anyway? He wouldn't even have been doing the tastings if Rachel hadn't sneaked them into his calendar. But then Sir Cuthbert—the senior partner in his firm, the man who held Will's career in his hands—had spotted Maya as she'd been on her way out of the building and Will had been forced into a corner.

Sir Cuthbert had arrived unannounced in Will's office.

'What have you done to Maya Hartney?'

No greetings, no small talk.

'What have I done to her?' Will had asked carefully. 'Nothing. Why? What did she say?'

By the time Will had admitted he hadn't tried even half the dishes Maya had brought with her he'd known that he was in trouble. Sir Cuthbert had had that look in his eye. The one that told Will he wouldn't want to hear what was coming next.

'I'm worried about you, Will.'

Not what he'd expected. And his concern wasn't necessary in the slightest.

'There's no need, Sir Cuthbert,' he'd said, relieved that he wasn't about to lose his job. 'I admit I was a little preoccupied in that meeting, and I'll make amends with Maya Hartney if I need to.' He made a mental note to have Rachel send her something.

'It's more than that, Will,' Sir Cuthbert had per-sisted. 'You don't take your holiday. You're always the last to leave the office. Some mornings I won-der whether you've been home at all.' He glanced down to the smartphone in Will's hand. 'You can't be parted from that thing for more than a minute. There's more to life and to *business* than the num-bers, Will. It's about people too. You need to take some time off or you're going to burn out.'

Will had suppressed a groan, impatient to get back to work, not interested in cod psychology from his boss. 'I'm grateful for your concern, Sir Cuthbert, really. But there isn't a problem. I don't need time off.'

'This isn't a request, Will.'

The older man crossed his arms and widened his stance, and for the first time Will realised he was serious. The man had no reason to question his commitment to his job. He put in twelve-, four-teen-, eighteen-hour days. Whatever it took to get the job done. He was more at home in his office than he was…well…at home. When he was there he was focussed. He tuned the world out, saw only his projects, the numbers. And now he was being reprimanded for spending *too much* time here.

'I mean it. If you don't take some time off I'm going to have some difficult choices to make about your role here. The pro bono work you're taking on, for example.'

'You can't make me drop the Julia House project, Cuthbert.' A swift shot of panic hit Will in the belly, but he pushed it away, determined to think this through logically, rationally. He smoothed back the sharp emotion until he couldn't feel it any longer; he didn't want to examine it or need to understand it. He just knew that ensuring the success of Julia House was an imperative. He had to make this work, so he focussed on fixing the problem.

'I don't want to, Will. I know it's a good cause, and I know it means a lot to you. But you're stressed and you're tired and today you took it out on Maya Hartney. Make it up to her. Fix the problem and take a few days to recharge, get some perspective. Or I'll have no choice but to cut back your non-essential work.'

How could he tell Sir Cuthbert that he hadn't been rude because he was stressed, or tired? He felt neither of those things. Throughout his life he'd trained himself to feel nothing. To manage his emotions—keep them at bay. He'd been rude to Maya because she had unsettled him, scared him, and putting distance between them had seemed the safest thing to do. Now he found himself standing on her doorstep, half hoping she wouldn't answer the door, worried about what it could lead to if she did.

Will wasn't sure what it was about her that had heated his blood and demanded his attention, but he'd had to force his eyes to his smartphone for the whole of their meeting just to keep any semblance of peace in his head. It had been years—more than a decade—since he'd last had to fight so hard to keep his cool.

He was used to meeting beautiful women. He was even used to taking beautiful women to bed. But he'd been blindsided by Maya's bright colours, her wild hair and the vulnerable anger in her eyes. He didn't want her in his head, and the gnawing feeling in his belly that had started when they met was disturbing. He was used to control. To taking what he wanted, giving what was desired and walking away with no one getting hurt. There was no reason to cede control here. She was just a little unusual. That was all. It was taking his brain a little longer to learn how to keep her at the same distance it did everything else.

Finally Maya came to the door. Back in the office he hadn't let himself really notice her appearance. But there it had been easier to stop himself, to pull his eyes back to his smartphone or the safe grey of the walls. Now he truly opened his eyes to appreciate her. The first thing he noticed, of course, were the colours. She was wearing *all* of them. He was far from an expert in these things, but was it normal to wear orange and pink together? Did one normally add yellow to that mix?

There was more to see than colour, though. His eyes followed the curves of her body, noticing the way her skirt spilt over her generous hips, swinging gently as she shifted her weight to one leg and waited for his gaze to reach her eyes. He knew that he should be looking away, shouldn't be indulging himself, allowing his guard to slip. But she fascinated him. Her very presence brought light and heat and energy. And, as much as he wanted those sensations gone, he couldn't help but pander to his curiosity.

When his gaze reached her face she raised an eyebrow. His appraisal hadn't gone unnoticed.

And it seemed that the attention was not appreciated. *Good.* He dragged his mind back to his work, back to Julia House. This was business and nothing else. There was no way that he could let Cuthbert pull his project. He had given his word that he would secure funding without fail, and if that meant persuading an errant chef to get back onside, regardless of the unsettling effect that she had on him, then that was what he would do.

He firmed his stance and squared his shoulders. He would make this right.

Maya opened the door wide, and as soon as she clocked him her face dropped into a scowl. Her hands rested on her hips, one of them wrapped tight around a wooden spoon. She was not expecting his visit, and he wasn't a welcome surprise. Well, good. He wasn't exactly thrilled to be here either.

Will braced himself. He had the horrible feeling that this was going to get messy. And he didn't *do* messy. Ever. He did cold and rational and detached, and he did it better than anyone else in the city. It was the only way to find any sense of peace. Looked as if she was going to make him grovel. And if he didn't he would have to deal with

Rachel's disapproving silence in the office tomorrow. When she'd heard Sir Cuthbert demand that he take time off she'd appeared in the doorway of his office with a flyer and a plan.

'Mr Thomas, I wasn't expecting you.' Maya brushed a smudge of flour from her cheek as she spoke.

'You wouldn't answer my emails, and we need to talk.' He knew that he sounded brusque—terse, even—but he wanted to stay focussed. Regardless of the constant threat of distraction, he needed to think strictly business to get this deal done.

Maya squared her shoulders, mirroring his confrontational stance, but then a beeping sound came from inside the cottage. She hesitated for a second, still eyeballing him, before turning and walking across the hallway.

'We can talk, if you insist,' she called over her shoulder, 'but I'm not going to change my mind and I'm not going to stop. I've got a sauce on the stove that won't wait.'

'Fine, fine.'

This hostile reaction had him on the back foot. He'd not expected this—not after her polite smiles in his office. But perhaps he'd underestimated the impact of his detachment. Perhaps she'd found those smiles harder to fake than he'd realised. He almost smiled himself—it would be so much easier to keep her at a distance when she was obviously keen to do the same. But he didn't like the thought that he might have hurt her. That he was the cause of that fine line of distress between her eyebrows.

He hated that she had him concerned, and thought that he might have exposed a vulnerability. A chink in her bright flowered armour. Because that would mean a connection between them— something they shared. Something that couldn't be undone or ignored.

He followed her through to the kitchen, his eyes drawn again to the shift of her skirt over her hips, the fabric clinging slightly to the curves of supple skin. He shook his head to clear his thoughts— again. This wasn't him. He was in his suit, working, and normally that was a guarantee that nothing distracted him. But this attraction was more than just an unwelcome distraction; it was a threat to his control and to the detachment that allowed him to function.

He dragged his eyes away just before she turned around.

'So, what can I help you with, Mr Thomas?'

Her tone was cool, and her manner no more friendly now that they were indoors. He was glad. It gave him every reason to respond with equal coolness. It kept her at a safe distance.

He spoke with cold, clipped tones the words that he'd rehearsed in the car. 'I understand from Rachel that you won't cater our function next month.'

'I won't.'

She turned away from the stove to face him head-on. The slight tremble in her clenched fists gave away her nerves, but her shoulders remained firm and he could see that she wouldn't back down from him easily. He'd had no idea at the time that his words, his actions, had had such an impact. But he could see no other reason that she would be so hostile towards him now.

'Can I ask why?' He ground the words out through clenched teeth and suspected even as he was saying them that he would regret doing so. A niggle of guilt had been eating away at him and he was starting to see why. He'd offended her—which was something he'd never intended. His standoff-ishness has been purely a defence mechanism.

Maya sighed, and from the way her shoulders tightened and she turned away from him to stir the sauce on the stove he guessed that she didn't enjoy conflict. Part of him was glad to have that insight; he saw a way to get what he wanted. If he pushed hard enough she'd back down just to avoid a fight.

She took a deep breath and then spoke. 'As I explained to Rachel, I don't think my food is right for your dinner. I think you will find another caterer who will better meet your needs.'

Her words sounded rehearsed, and though he was sure that she'd meant them to sound indifferent the edge to her voice and her vigorous beating of the sauce gave her away. Another twinge of guilt and a pang of fear fought for space in his belly. He'd had no idea that he'd hurt her feelings so much, and no real sense of how in jeopardy his project was until now.

He took a deep breath and tried to swallow the dry lump in his throat. 'I'm aware that I didn't give your food the attention it deserved when you came to the office, and I'm sorry that I was distracted during our meeting. We'd very much like to work with you.' He had to get this back on track, he thought, rubbing the back of his neck.

'Well, thank you for your apology,' she said, still refusing to look at him, 'but I'm afraid the answer's still no.'

'Why?' he persisted, his voice growing softer, though he hadn't intended it to. He was just changing tack, he told himself, just trying another way to get what he wanted. It didn't mean he wouldn't push her if he really needed to.

'Like I said, I don't think we're well suited. I don't think we'd work well together.'

She was still turned determinedly against him, her voice hard.

Will ran a hand through his hair, testing scenarios in his mind, trying to think objectively. Trying to find a rational, sensible business argument with which he could persuade her. 'Your food was fine,' he said, 'and I'm not asking you to work with me. I'm asking you to cater a dinner.'

'That proves my point exactly.' She whipped around and met his eye, brandishing her wooden spoon like a knife. Her voice and the colour in her face rose. 'Fine,' she said. 'You thought my food was *fine*.'

Partly he was pleased. Glad to have a reaction from her at last, thrilled that she was turning to face him. But mainly he was concerned about what this flash of anger meant for Julia House. He'd crafted a business argument that he was sure would put things right. And it had made things worse.

Maya turned back and continued to thrash at the sauce, hypnotising him with the way her skirt swung with every movement. It took a few seconds for his brain to catch up with his ears and eyes. What was wrong with *fine*? Nothing. There was no reason for him not to hire her, and no reason he could see for her to object to him. But though she'd pulled herself together he had seen hurt and anger cross her face. He didn't understand it, didn't understand why she had so much invested in this food of hers, but he didn't like that he'd upset her.

'Maya?' He wanted to leave. He didn't want to involve himself in whatever it was that made this woman turn down business because he'd described her food as 'fine'. But without her onside Sir Cuthbert could withdraw the company's support for the charity. He stayed put.

Maya took a breath and turned around, pasting on the smile that he recognised from his office.

'I'm sorry, but I can't cook for people who think my food is "fine". If I know you won't enjoy the food, I won't enjoy cooking it. If I don't enjoy cooking it, what's the point? The food won't be any good and I won't be happy.'

'Is this a general rule?' he asked. He forced a note of humour into his voice, hoping to lighten the mood.

The atmosphere in here was intense, and he could see from her tight muscles and hunched shoulders that Maya was a few wrong words away from an outburst that would put a permanent end to his project. Even putting that aside, he didn't want to see that happen. Being so close to such a volume of emotion made him uneasy; he could feel his own emotions welling up in response, weighing heavily against the door that kept them shut away.

'Do you always turn down business from people who don't gush over your food?' He tried to inject a little laughter, but his voice cracked and that door shifted when he saw the distress in her features.

'I don't know about a rule,' she said, her voice

weaker now, flat, as she stared down at the floor. 'It's never happened before.'

Will took a minute to think about this. He knew that he was the problem, and that the solution had to come from him. But he was trying desperately to see a way out of the plan that Rachel and Cuthbert had pincered him into. There had to be something. Because the thought of having to go through with it tightened his chest until he struggled to breathe.

'Look, Maya. I know we don't exactly see eye to eye on this; I don't appreciate food like you do.' He took a deep breath, tried to steady his voice. 'But what if I was prepared to learn?'

He regretted the words immediately. He knew that as much as he would try to fight off the memories being back in a kitchen, oohing and aahing over delicious treats, would be close to torture.

'What do you mean?' She turned around and looked at him, surprise in her voice and on her face.

'Back at the office you told Rachel that you're running a cookery course next week, and that there was a space free. If I take the course, try to connect with your food, will you reconsider?' He controlled his fear and his voice, but if he'd had any other choice, if this was any other project, he'd be running from here—from her—as fast as he could.

She eyed him carefully, her head tilted to one side. 'I'm not sure.'

She turned to face him. The anger and the tension had left her stance, and instead she studied his face. The tightness in his chest lightened.

'And that space is gone anyway. The client called me—they managed to find someone to fill it.'

'Well, can't you run it with one extra?'

Maya shook her head and went back to her sauce, stirring more gently now. But Will didn't make a move to leave. He had to get her to agree, somehow, and she looked as if she might be thinking it over, reconsidering. Eventually, she spoke.

'I can't. There's not enough space in the kitchen and it wouldn't be fair on the other students. If you're serious, though—if you really want to learn—I have some time the following week. I'll have to fit in some development and planning work, but if you're happy to work around that I can run another course.'

He gulped. 'One on one?'

'One on one.'

CHAPTER TWO

MAYA FIDDLED WITH her necklace as the car door slammed and forced her feet to the floor, determined not to be waiting for him at the door. This was a bad idea. The hurt she'd felt in his office was something she'd thought she was long past. The feeling of rejection was something she'd not felt since she'd last seen her parents. But after an hour in this man's company self-doubt had been needling her non-stop.

If it hadn't been for the flash of fear and hurt she'd recognised in his eyes—well hidden, but still just visible—she'd have turned him down again. But in the face of his desperation, and her curiosity, she'd known she had to think of some way to help him. And perhaps if she could get him here, get him to enjoy her food, those doubts would fade. Her faith in the joy she could bring with her food could blossom again.

She tidied away the last of her lunch dishes and

surveyed the kitchen. It was always spotless, of course, but this morning, with summer in the air, it seemed to glow more than usual. It had been carefully designed to balance the charmingly old and the strikingly modern—the stainless steel of a professional grill with rich, warm Cotswold stone and aged oak beams. Perhaps the charm of the old cottage would mellow him, she pondered nervously.

Nervous anticipation spread through her body at the thought of being alone in the house with the man who had so riled and frustrated her. Their last two meetings had left her unsettled, and she knew that she was gambling with her emotions, with the happy life and the confidence that she had built for herself, and couldn't quite recall why she had suggested this.

Because when he had come to her, asking her to reconsider, she'd seen a glimpse of something in his eyes that had made her pause—just for a second he'd seemed vulnerable. So different from the coolness she'd felt in his office—and she was curious. She had also seen what he'd been trying so hard to hide—he needed her. He was desperate for her help. And she'd found that she couldn't say no, whatever it might cost her.

And then she remembered how he had looked at her, his wide eyes skimming her, almost in disbelief…how her mouth had watered and her lips had tingled at the sight of him…and she suspected she might have had an ulterior motive.

She hadn't been able to stop thinking about him in the days since they'd met. To start with it had been easy to ignore her attraction, to concentrate instead on her hurt and her anger at the way he had completely rejected her food—and, by extension, her. But since he'd come to her door, begged her to reconsider, she hadn't been able to get those silver eyes out of her mind, trying to work out what was beneath.

The doorbell rang and she knew that it was too late for doubts and worries. She would make this work.

Smoothing back her hair, she forced her shoulders down and went to answer the door.

'Will, welcome to Rose Cottage.' He flinched as she said the words, and she had to school her features not to reflect it back to him. Acting on instinct, she reached out and placed a hand on his arm to reassure him. She hated to see anyone distressed, ached to make things right. But he pulled away from her abruptly, shock and annoyance on his face. She cringed; she'd only been trying to help and he'd rejected her. Again.

Now, of course, she was questioning the wisdom of having him here more than ever. But she had a chance to make this cold, indifferent man fall in love with food, to make his world a brighter, more joyful place, and she couldn't resist it.

And the plan had one other redeeming feature, she supposed: Will was pretty easy on the eye. He wore another grey suit today—Maya doubted he owned any other colour—and a crisp white shirt, open at the neck. She guessed that he'd come straight from the office, no matter that it was a Sunday, and he had the look of a man who spent too many hours staring at a computer screen. But the austerity of his clothes highlighted the sharp steel of his eyes and the hint of shadow below his cheekbones. A calculating look came over those grey eyes then, and she could practically see the cogs turning as he tried to turn the situation to his advantage.

She looked over the evidence of his apprehension: set shoulders, grim face, flat voice. She realised that she was never going to convince him of the joys of her cuisine if they were both approaching the week like this. One of them would have to make the effort to brighten the mood in here. She'd pasted on a happy face often enough before; she could do it now.

There was no getting away from it: he was gorgeous. She'd noticed it the first time she'd set eyes on him. But even with those sharply defined cheekbones, the hint of stubble, the lips she was dying to taste, there was one flaw she couldn't overlook. He just wasn't quite...*there*. Any time she'd sensed she might be getting a look at the real Will Thomas, every time a conversation took a turn away from the strictly rational and objective, he'd disappeared into himself in an instant.

Sometimes the shutters just slammed down. At other times they wavered long enough for her to see something lingering—a tiny suggestion of past hurts, perhaps, that had made him the way he was. Whatever it was that she'd glimpsed, it was enough for her to know that getting involved would be bad news

She'd spent the first eighteen years of her life

devoid of affection, lacking warmth and love. She'd been an unwelcome surprise to older parents, shunted from nannies to boarding school and back again, and she had never stopped trying to impress them, never stopped hoping that one day she'd make them proud.

Even when she'd gone to a prestigious university, as they had, and completed her history degree, as she'd thought they'd wanted, it hadn't been enough for them. Her whole life she'd been a disappointment to them. But when she'd discovered her passion for food, the joy that she could bring to her housemates and friends with her cooking, she'd also found the warm glow she could create in a room. She wanted, *needed*, to live her life among people who were happy and contented, and she'd do everything she could to make those around her feel that way. So she'd used the money her parents had given her—she would have swapped it in a heartbeat for genuine affection, but that was the one thing they'd never offered—to start her culinary training and then her business.

She couldn't, *wouldn't*, allow herself to develop feelings for someone who was never going to be able to return them.

* * *

'So, are you ready for this?'

Maya eyed the knives laid out on the scrubbed oak countertop and wondered if this had been the wisest move. It looked as if she had some sort of medieval torture lined up for them, and from the resigned, stoic set of Will's face she could see that he was expecting nothing less. She didn't like the thought of hurting him, and wondered again whether she was doing the right thing? But he had come to her wanting to learn, and she was determined to help, to bring him happiness.

'I thought we'd start with something simple. So we're going to cut a fillet from this fish—' she gestured, smiling tentatively, to where she'd laid two gleaming fresh fish in a bowl of ice '—and then make a herb butter. It'll be delicious.'

She'd hoped that some of her enthusiasm might rub off, but Will didn't look convinced. His fingers were curled into tight fists and she could see the tension all the way up his arms to his shoulders. His eyes darted around the kitchen, before fixing on a spot in mid-air.

She looked up at Will's face, trying to see how he had reacted to her suggestion. So far, no change.

But she'd no choice but to plough on and hope that her gamble would pay off.

'Here.' She handed him the fish and the filleting knife and showed him how to clean and gut it. 'What you need to do next...'

She started to explain, and caught Will's eye as she looked up. He was watching her intently. Well, he might not be connecting with the food, she thought, but he did look determined to get this right. That was a start at least.

'What you need to do next is feel for the spine through the flesh and just let the blade glide along that line.'

The look on his face told her that he was determined to follow her instructions, but the way he was gripping the knife made her nervous.

'Just relax your hand,' she said. 'The knife is sharp, so you just need to guide it and let it do the work.'

He grimaced as he forced the point of the knife into the fish. He was overthinking it, trying to push the knife where he thought it should be going rather than responding to the feel of it in his hand.

'Wait,' Maya cautioned him gently, taking in his fierce expression and white knuckles; she didn't want him to slip and cut himself. 'You just need to be patient with it. Don't rush.' She moved closer to his side and laid her hand over his, easing his fingers back from where they were gripping the knife. 'Loosen your hand.'

Will did as he was told, and suddenly Maya was aware of how much closer she'd moved. The whole of the left side of her body was pressed against him, and her right arm, reaching across her body to help Will hold the knife, was doing something outrageous to her cleavage. She looked up and saw that Will had just made the same realisation. The red flush spreading over her face and chest added another colour to that day's collection.

She tried to step away from him, hoping that she hadn't given away evidence of her attraction. The last thing she needed was him guessing about the feelings she was trying to chase away. She didn't want them—knew that acting on her attraction was bound to lead to hurt.

As she moved away she felt the knife slip, and knew before it happened that it was heading straight for her index finger.

'Ouch!' she yelped as the blade nicked her skin.

She tried to draw her hand away, but sliced deeper into her knuckle in the process.

Concern clouded Will's face as he reached for her hand. 'Are you okay?'

Maya tried to pull back; being close to him was too tempting, too good to be safe. But he took a gentle hold of her wrist as he examined the cut.

'I'm fine, really.'

She pulled her hand from his, wanting to clear her head. He was making it impossible to think clearly. All she wanted was a little space, a little distance between them. But he kept moving closer. His face still screamed grim determination, only this time *she* was the subject. He would help her whether she wanted it or not. When he was standing so close to her, showing such concern for a little cut, she had to remind herself of what she'd realised out in the hallway. Indulging that flutter in her belly and the racing in her pulse when she looked at Will Thomas was a very bad idea. Nothing was guaranteed to hurt her like indifference did. And she knew first-hand Will Thomas's capacity for that.

She headed for the first aid box she kept by the sink.

'At least I didn't bleed on the fish.' There was a little shake in her voice as she realised the strength of her feelings and the depth of her vulnerability. 'It'll still be okay for dinner. And you were doing a great job before I slipped.'

'*You* were doing great,' Will corrected her.

She turned to look at him, taken aback by the gravelly tone of his voice. His face showed more distress than ever, and she wondered why.

'You were fine; you just need to loosen up a little.' She spoke guardedly, protecting her feelings and his. With one hand under the tap, she tried to open the catch on the first aid box.

'Let me do that,' Will said, walking over to her.

She tried to insist that she could manage, but he washed his hands and then pulled the box from out of her reach. When he turned back he had gauze, blue plasters and a bandage in his hands and a determined look back on his face.

'Will, I think just the plaster will probably do it.' Maya risked a chuckle, hoping that it would break the tension in the air, but Will ignored her and stepped closer.

'Stop, Maya. Why is it so hard to let me help you? You don't have to do it all yourself.'

What other way was there? She'd done everything for herself all her life. And then spent most
of her adult life doing whatever she could for other
people. No one had ever tried to take care of *her*
before.

She looked up at him and forgot everything
she had told herself about not letting him close.
Lost every self-protective instinct she had nur-
tured since stepping into his office. He just walked
straight through every barrier she'd erected, every
promise she'd made to herself since they'd met.
Instead of getting away, she wondered how she'd
not noticed before how tall he was—another
inch closer and he'd be able to rest his chin on
her head—and explored the structure of his face
from this new, sharper angle.

His eyes didn't leave her face, though they
darted between her eyes and her mouth as he
reached across and turned off the tap. His forehead wrinkled and his eyes were serious as he
wrapped gauze around her finger, applying pressure as he pulled her hand between them, and then
reached for a paper towel. He scrutinised the cut,
watching the red beads bloom from her skin, and

then clamped the gauze down. Maya gave a little gasp of discomfort.

'Sorry,' Will said, and she saw that his concern was genuine. 'But the pressure will stop it bleeding.'

She knew that, of course, but she couldn't help wondering whether that was really why he was standing so close, why neither of them had taken a step back. She told herself that he was only so close because he was helping her. But she knew that she was kidding herself. She'd been drawn to him from the first time she'd met him, and it was only her rigid determination to protect herself that had stopped her imagining this intimacy before. She wasn't sure that she had the strength to pull away now that she was here. She took a deep breath to steady the swimming sensation that threatened to make her sway.

When Will was satisfied the cut had stopped bleeding he carefully unwrapped a plaster and pressed it around her finger, catching her eye as he did so and watching her expression. Smoothing the edges down, he inspected the digit from several angles, ensuring that the plaster held firm, and then held it up for her approval.

'Thanks.' The word came out breathy, unsure, and as she heard her voice she knew that she had to act. She had to do something—and now—if she was going to stop herself getting hurt. This had gone more than far enough already. Maya looked up from her finger to Will's face. 'It's fine now,' she said, trying to pull her hand away.

But Will kept a firm hold on it, using it to pull her fractionally closer until her chest was pressed against him.

And then he froze. Maya watched reality crash through his face as he realised what he was doing. He dropped her hand and turned away from her, and she glimpsed his hard, set expression twist into a grimace.

Relief and disappointment flooded Maya and she leant back against the sink, trying to remember that space was what she had wanted. But his rejection stung her nonetheless. She kept her eyes on the floor until she could look up at him with an indifferent expression.

'Let's carry on,' she managed eventually.

Will proceeded to hack the remains of the fillet from the fish. She briefly considered trying to help, but her last attempt had ended in a sliced finger. By the look of the way he was handling the knife this time around, if she tried to interfere now she was likely to lose a hand. For the first time she could remember she wished she wasn't in her kitchen. She wished she could escape upstairs, hide away from this man and the dangerous effect he had on her. But she'd committed to help him and she wouldn't go back on her word.

Things didn't improve when she tried to explain the sauce. She'd hoped that a simple herb butter would be a good way for him to become familiar with the flavours of the different herbs from the kitchen garden behind the house. But his response when she suggested that he smelt and tasted each one was 'nice' or 'fine'. And the increasing detachment in his gaze showed him retreating further from her with every prompt, shutting her out just a little bit tighter.

In the end, with her finger and her feelings hurting more than she wanted to admit, she decided she just wanted the day over with and gave up any pretence of trying to reach him. The sooner it was ready, the sooner they could eat, and then she could escape this stifling atmosphere that had invaded her home.

This wasn't what her kitchen was for. She loved to share her passion with other people. Help them to discover a new talent, or develop a skill, or just eat chocolate pudding until they couldn't move if that was what brought them pleasure. This room existed to make people happy, created the bliss that she needed to fend off the memories of her childhood. Or it had until this man had walked in here, all taciturn and cold, and brought her decades-old insecurities with him.

With a final addition of salt and pepper she decided that the food was as good as it was going to get, considering the mood of the chefs, and set it on warm plates. She and Will carried the food and a bottle of chilled white wine to the table outside, and Maya wondered how they were going to get through this dinner. Will had said barely five words since they'd left the sink, and if she allowed it to the silence would become unbearable.

But what could they talk about?

Maya wished that she'd thought this through before she'd agreed to run the course for him. She loved to talk about food. When people found out that she was a cook they always asked about her work, and she was happy to talk shop for as long as they would put up with her. But she suspected that food would not be high on Will's list of favourite topics of conversation. In fact she wondered if he had ever had a conversation about food that hadn't involved a consideration of gross profit.

Silence. It was definitely not golden. It was bad-tempered and it was awkward and it was the final insult for a much-abused meal.

She gazed out over the meadow beyond the garden, hoping that the view, which never normally failed to cheer her, would have its usual soothing effect. The shadows of the clouds chased over the ground, causing the colours of the wildflowers to shift and change, and the corners of her lips twitched upwards. She encouraged it into a full-blown smile as she let the beauty and serenity of her home topple her bad temper.

She'd fallen in love with the view, and this house, the moment that she'd first seen them. It was exactly what she'd needed: somewhere to escape from the slick city kitchens she had been working in until then, to get away from the constant client pitches, the networking events. And so she'd created a haven here—somewhere she could experience the intense colours and fresh scents of the natural world, could be completely creative. And she'd made herself part of the community. Here she understood what she needed to do, how to make people happy.

She'd thought she'd known what she was getting when she'd paid for the old stone house and its beautiful garden. And then the place had sprung a surprise on her.

The first cookery class she'd run had been a complete accident: she'd invited faithful clients to come for the weekend and sample her new menu, not long after having her professional kitchen installed. She'd been sure no one else would feel quite the same thrill she did at the sight of her new oven, but she'd wanted to show it off anyway.

Except once her guests had arrived they hadn't been content just to sit and watch her cook for them. They had all wanted to muck in, despite the fact that not one of them had known how to chop an onion. They'd pushed her to let them help, and she'd realised that cooking wasn't the only thing that could make her glow. Teaching was another way of sharing her food, and her love of food, with others. Before the weekend was over they'd practically written her business plan for her, and she'd found herself with a teaching business alongside her cooking.

And now Will was threatening that thrill as well. Every time he turned his nose up at her food he impugned her teaching as well as her cooking.

But the beautiful view boosted her. She'd bloomed when she'd come here from the city, when her world had shrunk and she'd finally found a place for herself. Maybe Will just needed a little of that magic. He'd charged her with teaching him, and she wasn't going to give up just because of his bad temper.

As she gazed off into the distance she realised that putting space between her and Will, constantly pulling away from him, was going to doom their experiment from the start. How could she expect him to open up and appreciate what was around him if she was sitting there trying to pretend that he *wasn't* there?

She drew her gaze back from the meadow and fixed it on Will's face. The expression in his eyes was serious, focussed, and it intrigued her. She wondered what thoughts lay behind those silver-grey eyes, where he went when he retreated like this. Tracing her gaze over his features, she followed the line of his straight, narrow nose to lips that looked almost too full, too sumptuous, with his slim face and sharp features.

He slid his knife through the fish in neat, straight lines, carving it methodically. She watched, intrigued, his precise, emotionless approach, and fought down her instinct to look for approval. Her feelings when she served someone her food were always the same. Did they like it? Of course Will's face gave her no hint. She had to force down the disappointment that he showed no pleasure in it. Tell herself that this was still early days. But she couldn't stop herself hoping. Just a few small genuine words from him would soothe her fears, show her that they were on the right track. Ease the pain that the rejection of their first meeting had caused.

Will seemed to sense her staring at him, because he glanced up and held her gaze for a moment, before remembering what manners required of him.

'This is nice, thank you.'

Maya sighed; they still had a lot of work to do—not least on thickening her skin. But they had to start somewhere, and if she wanted him to be open with her, to open himself to the joy that she hoped her food would bring, she would have to show him the way. She should see each barb as an opportunity—he had come to her for help, and each sting would tell her how much work they still had to do.

She glanced across at the meadow, letting the colours and the glory of the sunset sink into her skin and smooth away this latest hurt. Eventually she turned to Will, trying to reflect those rays of evening sun back to him.

'So, Will, why don't you tell me more about your work?'

He met her eyes again, and she watched his face for clues, signs that he was making progress. But all she saw was him bracing himself, hardening his eyes and fixing a neutral expression. All that for small talk, she thought, and wondered what pain lingered behind the façade to make it such a frightening prospect.

'My company offers a range of financial services,' he said, his voice flat and clipped. 'At the moment I'm working on a project to raise funds for a health sector construction scheme.' A frown creased his brow and he looked troubled…tired. 'But I won't bore you with the details.'

'I'm not bored,' she said. 'I wouldn't have asked if I wasn't interested. I'd like to understand more about your work. It's a charity fundraiser, the dinner you want me to cater, isn't it? Do you do a lot of work with charities?'

'No.'

As she watched she could see him trying to distance himself further. He looked away, past her shoulder, and plucked his phone from his jacket pocket. She suspected he didn't even realise that he'd done it. One-sided small talk was its own particular form of torture, and without his help she had no idea how to steer this conversation onto safer ground. She stumbled for words, not wanting them to end the evening on an awkward silence, hoping for even the tiniest breakthrough. She decided to stick with business questions—maybe if they could get comfortable talking about that, they could progress from there.

'So, is it interesting, working with a charity? What type of charity is it? How did you get involved?'

Perhaps if she just kept throwing questions out there one of them would stick. But at the last one Will dropped his fork, placed his elbow on the table and rested his head in his hand.

Will looked…broken. More pain than she'd seen

one person bear weighed heavy in his eyes and on his shoulders, and she hated that she'd caused that. Regret curled in her belly at the knowledge that she'd brought someone so much grief. This week was meant to be about pleasure, about learning to appreciate flavour and beauty and art. But from the way that his elbows had come up onto the table to turn him in on himself, shield his body, she knew that she'd made a huge error.

Her instincts told her to move closer, but his body language screamed *Keep Out*. She rested her hands flat on the table to stop herself reaching across to him. Seeing Will like this threw everything that she'd thought she knew about him into new light. She'd seen hints of something haunting him, but had never imagined that he was carrying such raw pain.

'Will…?' She didn't want to make this worse; she only wanted to help.

'It's a hospice,' he said quietly. 'I have a…a family connection to it.'

'Oh.'

She knew that the response was inadequate. His few words, forced out through gritted teeth, had carried a great weight of buried hurt. There was so much she didn't know about him, but with those words she'd started to understand him a little more. No wonder he was distant, if *this* was what threatened when he opened up. No wonder he eyed her with distrust and trepidation when she wanted emotion from him.

'I'm sorry,' she said, caving in to her instincts and touching his hand. 'It's none of my business.'

'It's fine.' Will picked up his fork, shrugging off her touch, and his face was smoothed over.

Maya guessed that he was fighting against memories, and winning this time.

'Julia, my foster mother, died fifteen years ago. One of her nurses started a hospice charity and asked me to provide financial advice.' He spoke with an angry edge to his voice, apparently still fighting for control.

'Oh,' she said again. It was still inadequate.

'I don't want to talk about it,' Will said, solving her dilemma. 'Not now. Not ever.'

Maya lay in bed and checked the clock on her bedside table. Still only five o'clock. A little early to be crashing around when she had a guest in the house, especially one who'd seemed so annoyed with her by the time they'd gone upstairs last night. After her disastrous attempt at small talk Will had swept up the dishes from the table and clattered around in the kitchen, tidying up. She'd followed him, wanting to help—with the dishes, with his pain—but he'd scowled at her when she'd walked through the door and told her that he could manage. She'd started to argue, to insist that he didn't need to, but the glare that he'd sent in her direction had had her retracing her steps out through the door. She'd watched through the window as she picked up the last few things from the table, had seen the blank look in his eyes. He'd scrubbed at the counters, cleaning them in long straight strokes, and she guessed that he'd found some comfort in those actions.

She'd known beyond doubt that her presence in the kitchen would upset him further. It didn't matter how much she wanted to apologise, to put things right, he'd needed her to stay away.

When he'd finally gone upstairs she'd wished him goodnight and told him she'd see him back down here in the morning; then she'd sorted through the last few things in the kitchen before following him up. As she'd reached the landing she'd heard frantic typing, fingers being hammered into a keyboard, and had let out a long sigh. This week was already proving to be so much harder than she'd ever dreamt, and this was only day one. Will had asked her to teach him, but she was worried that he would fight the temptation to learn with his last breath.

Lying in bed was doing her no good this morning. She'd woken so many times through the night, thinking about the disastrous evening in the kitchen and on the terrace—she couldn't have slept for more than an hour at a time.

Making this week a success had never seemed less likely than it did this morning. But Will had laid down the gauntlet, challenged her to teach him, and she was determined to see it through. He was here, and there was something in that simple fact that made Maya want to persevere. This man needed happiness in his life, something to balance the grief she had glimpsed last night, and the only thing she knew that could deliver joy of that magnitude was food.

She wouldn't push. She couldn't force something that he didn't feel. All she could do was make her food so irresistible that he couldn't help but enjoy it. And her sleepless night had given her plenty of time to think about how to go about it. This morning she wouldn't ask Will to cook. She would just surround him with delicious smells and tastes, lighten his mood and help him feel relaxed in the kitchen.

She dragged her tired body out of bed and into the shower, making plans in her head for something that would reach out and bring Will a little relief. Perhaps something with fresh fruit? That way it would introduce him to more of her garden. Or something spiced that would appeal to the nose as well as the palate?

After blasting her hair with the dryer she selected her pinkest, floweriest, summeriest dress from the wardrobe. For someone with as much red hair as she had it was not an obvious choice of colour, but she was going to exude sunshine and pleasure today. Will had been in her house a day, and seemed even less happy than he had when he'd arrived. She couldn't allow herself to take a step back; if she was going to make this work she had to throw everything she could at it.

She hunted frantically for ingredients, looking for inspiration in the walk-in fridge, grabbing fruit and butter, eggs and milk. She whipped and beat and whisked and folded, and every time she slid another tray into the oven she reached for a mixing bowl again. The familiar actions chased last night's shadows out of the kitchen and she breathed more easily as she saw the results of her work piling up on the countertops. This would work. This had to work. There had to be *something* here that would get through to him.

She threw the switch on her food mixer, adjusted the oven temperature, turned cakes out onto racks. A simple sponge, shortbread, scones, pizza bases. She found spiced cream, home-made jams and fresh berries. Perfect for building layers of flavours.

She picked at the fruit and munched on biscuits as she went. With her recent late nights, and the stress of a student who didn't want to learn, she was asking for a migraine. Lucky for her, keeping her blood sugar up and cooking out her stress were the best ways to fend one off.

And when at last the huge container of flour was empty she leaned back against the counter and surveyed her work. Spoons, spatulas and whisks were stacked up by the sink. Her supply of mixing bowls was exhausted and every inch of counter space was covered with the evidence or the fruits of her labour.

Some of it she barely remembered making. She hadn't been thinking. She'd just let her hands and her heart take over her body.

She thought of Will's fingers stroking the screen of his phone, hammering on his laptop last night, and couldn't help but recognise the similarities. She'd reached for comfort this morning, as she'd seen him do.

There was more food here than she and Will could eat in a month, never mind a week. It could go in the freezer once it cooled, she thought, mentally flicking through her diary for the next couple of weeks. She had a couple of afternoon teas booked that the cakes and biscuits would be perfect for.

She glanced at the clock. It was gone ten o'clock already and she'd seen no sign of Will yet. Oh, well, he wouldn't be the first hardened workaholic to succumb to the effects of country air. She'd plan for elevenses and if there was no sign of him by then she'd knock on his door, just to make sure everything was okay. *Unless he's not in his room,* she thought to herself, and her spoon dropped to the counter with a clatter.

What if he had left already? Decided that whatever she was trying to teach him wasn't worth sticking around for?

A stab of pain slid through her belly as memories of being just not good enough surfaced. Weekends spent in an empty house because her parents had had more important things to do, or long summer holidays spent at school because she wasn't wanted at home. She'd thought that those feelings were long gone. Until she'd met Will Thomas she'd not thought of those times for years, but now… He had rejected her once. It would be so easy for him to do it again.

The hollow feeling of fear curled in her stomach and she rushed to the front door, relieved to see Will's car still parked on the drive. He was still here. That had to count for something. She still had a chance.

She couldn't quite rationalise her relief, given how frustrating yesterday had been. But, however difficult it was proving to be, she needed to help him. She couldn't look at someone in pain, someone who needed help, and simply do nothing. And then there was the spark that she'd felt between them when he'd bandaged her finger. The tender concern he'd shown her. The way that he'd started to pull her close before getting spooked. The fact that he'd pushed her away almost immediately should have been enough to tell her that she would have been better off if he'd gone.

'Everything all right?' Will appeared at the top of the stairs dressed in grey trousers and another crisp white shirt, phone in hand.

'Everything's fine,' Maya said, not wanting him to guess what she'd been thinking. 'I thought I heard the doorbell.'

She gestured widely with her arm towards the front door from where she stood at the bottom of the stairs. Turning her body towards him, she rested her hands on her hips and smiled up at him.

'Did the country air knock you out?'

'No, no. I've been up for a while. I was going to come and find you, actually,' Will said.

He was looking for her? Warmth spread through her body at that thought, chasing away the cold she'd felt a second ago when she'd thought he might have left. She was so overwhelmed with relief that he hadn't walked away, hadn't rejected her as she'd thought, that she didn't step back from the stairs as he descended. Even when he reached the bottom and was standing just a few inches away. Instead she enjoyed the feeling of being close to him, the way the air between them almost hummed. Like yesterday, those few good moments in a sea of disaster, when he'd shown such concern for the little cut on her finger.

The memory of the cold that had followed as he'd walked away was not, apparently, enough to make her body stop wanting him.

'You were?'

'Yes, my battery's about to die and I've forgotten my charger.' He poked at the screen of his phone and then gave a long sigh. 'I have a conference call in ten minutes. I don't suppose there's a spare one around here anywhere?'

Maya gulped, trying not to show her anger. He was working. He'd probably been up at the crack of dawn, as she had. But whereas she'd spent hours in the kitchen, trying to figure out how they were going to make this experiment of theirs work, he'd been happily ensconced in his room, getting on with business as normal. He hadn't even bothered to tell her what he was doing that morning. He'd just got on with his day without giving her a single thought.

Maya felt a chill sink through her as the implications hit home. She had spent all morning trying to make his day better in a small way, even if all she had to offer him was cake. She knew that it couldn't possibly fix his pain. But she'd tried. She'd thrown everything at helping him the only way she knew how. And he'd not thought of her at all. He couldn't have made it any clearer how little she, her food or her time meant to him.

She took a step back as her shoulders slumped, and her arms came across her body, protecting her from further blows.

'That's not a problem, is it?' Will ran a hand through his hair and it came to rest of the back of his neck.

Maya picked up on the tension in his body, the sharper edge to his voice. He'd sensed he'd upset her, she guessed, and was looking for an escape route.

'I'm sorry; I didn't think you'd need me in the kitchen until this evening. You didn't mention last night...'

Actually, she had mentioned it last night, but he

clearly hadn't been listening. And she shouldn't have to force him. His attendance on the course had been *his* idea. He was the one who had said that he wanted to learn—or that he was prepared to try, at least. And if that was the case then he had to be proactive. He had to make an effort—not just show up when he thought it was unavoidable.

She clenched her fist against the anger building in her—at herself as well as at him. All morning. She'd spent all morning trying to make this idea of his work, and he hadn't even bothered to turn up.

This thought, heaped on top of disappointment, sparked anger—at Will, at her parents, at herself—and she knew that they couldn't continue like this. Every day that she was around Will she was reminded that she'd never been enough. When her food wasn't working for her she felt unworthy of his, *anyone's* attention. She wasn't helping him; all she was doing was hurting them both. He would be better off leaving.

Maya tried to keep the heartbreak from her voice, reminding herself that really this was just business. 'I think we need to talk. I'll be waiting for you in the kitchen.' She didn't bother looking to see Will's reaction but stalked through the door and let it slam behind her. She knew that she hadn't succeeded. Her words had been sharp, clipped, forced out so that her voice wouldn't waver. But she knew that she hadn't fooled him into thinking they were detached.

When Will walked into the kitchen she recognised the determination on his face—he was obviously worried that he had blown his chance with her, and with good reason. She couldn't take any more of his cutting insults, whether he knew that he was making them or not.

'Oh, I didn't realise you'd started already. You should have shouted if you needed my help.' He ran a hand through his hair as he took in the array of baked goods cooling on the counter.

A flush of colour crept up Maya's neck as she tried to rein in her frustration and embarrassment—her every feeling was laid bare on the worktops of her kitchen. Hours of love and hope had been poured into cake tins, lined up carefully on baking trays, and there was no hiding from the passion that was displayed on every side.

'I didn't need your help, Will,' she snapped. As if it wasn't bad enough that she was wearing her heart on her sleeve, showing him how important

he was to her—something she hadn't quite realised herself before this moment—he'd completely missed the point. 'I'm perfectly capable
of doing it myself. But why weren't you here? This
week was *your* idea. You committed to doing it.
But all I'm getting from you is half-measures.
You're wasting my time as well as yours, and I
think you should pack your bags and go.'

She watched as her words registered and knew
that she had shocked him. For a minute he actually relaxed and leaned back against the counter,
his eyes wide as he watched her. She could understand why. She almost wished she could see herself from the outside right now, because she didn't
recognise the person who had just spoken. Maya
was always nice. It was who she was—what she
did every day. Making people happy. She wasn't
sure that she'd *ever* lost her temper and spoken to
someone the way she'd just hissed at him.

She was surprised at how good it felt—it was
exhilarating. There was a freedom in it that she'd
never felt before. If her food meant nothing to him,
then she had nothing else to offer. He couldn't
make her feel any worse than he had just now, so
what did she have to lose?

She held her ground, refusing to look away as he continued to stare at her, and she guessed that he was weighing up his options. She felt sure that he wanted to go, that he was here under duress of some sort, because he surely wasn't enjoying it. Watching him, she could tell that it was complicated. There was more to his insistence on her catering for him, more to him being here, than he'd told her, but would that reason outweigh his desire to get away?

'I'm sorry,' he said eventually. 'I'm here to learn; I'm committed to this.'

Apparently it would. But if he thought that was a decent apology, he was mistaken. She crossed her arms a little harder across her chest and tilted her head, waiting for him to continue.

'I didn't sleep,' he said at last, 'after what we talked about last night. But I shouldn't have taken that out on you. This is very important to me.'

There was no faking that sort of sincerity, she thought, noting the way his voice was carefully controlled—presumably to stop it breaking. She might be angry. She was *definitely* angry. But that didn't make her insensible to his feelings. Will was hurting.

'I'd need you to make a real effort,' she told him. 'You need to decide right now whether you're going to take this seriously. If not, I'll pack your bags for you.'

Will eyed her warily but she stopped herself from taking her words back, from apologising. Instead she waited. Waited to see what effect her words would have when she didn't care what the listener thought of her. When she had nothing to lose.

'I didn't expect things to get so…personal, but from now on no half-measures,' he said. 'I *will* do this. Properly.'

Apparently brutal honesty got her what she wanted.

She watched him force a smile onto his face. She would have preferred to see a genuine one, but she liked that he was trying. And she thought that maybe there was still a chance that she could help him, as he'd asked.

'Okay. We'll try again. But you might want to lose the suit—change into something that doesn't need dry cleaning,' she added. If he was willing to try she would give him another chance. If nothing else it would be an interesting challenge to try and teach someone so different from her usual clients. At least that was what she could tell herself. It was nothing to do with the spark she felt between them; nothing to do with exploring this new-found bravado and honesty. Nothing to do with the way her body craved being close to his.

CHAPTER THREE

THREE MINUTES LATER Will appeared in the doorway dressed in jeans and a black T-shirt.

Definitely an improvement, Maya decided, her eyes lingering on the contours of his upper arms. She was determined to start afresh, to put all thoughts of their argument and her hurt aside. His hands were in his pockets, but his arms appeared stiff, belying his façade of calm. His jaw was tense, his mouth pulled into a hard line. But Maya forced herself to look away, to paint a smile on her own face and hope that soon she would see it reflected in his.

'Ready to get started?' she asked, in a sunny, breezy voice. She wondered whether her own attempt to cover up her feelings was any more successful than his.

'Sure,' Will replied, not quite keeping the apprehension out of his voice, but she appreciated the effort.

Maya forced another smile and loaded cakes and biscuits onto a tray. 'I thought we'd sit outside as it's such a lovely day.'

She headed out to the terrace, where the sunlight broke through the leaves of the trees, throwing mottled patches of light onto the tablecloth and making the sugar atop her biscuits glisten. She set the tray on the table, beside a pot of tea and bowls of fruit. Finally, with all her tools in place, she took a seat opposite Will.

'Right, this is elevenses...' She checked her watch. 'Or near enough. You'll probably be pleased to hear that this doesn't involve actual cooking.' She'd rehearsed the words in her head when he'd disappeared upstairs to change, but now she stopped, taking in the blank look in his eyes and realising she'd lost him already.

'Elevenses?'

'Elevenses. Tea and cake taken around eleven in the morning.' She said. 'The preserve of grandmothers everywhere.'

'But you're not a grandmother,' Will pointed out, and she was surprised to see him relax a little, perhaps even a hint of amusement in his eyes as they met hers and wouldn't look away.

She smiled in return, relieved that the tension between them was lifting, and couldn't help wondering whether there was anything else to see in those eyes. Whether maybe some of the attraction she'd been fighting off since she'd met him was reflected there too. Her heart lurched at that thought; it had been hard enough keeping her own feelings at bay—knowing that he might feel the same would make it so much worse, so much more dangerous.

'You're right. I don't even *have* a grandmother. But I do love tea and cake. So here we are.'

'Fine. Good. Elevenses,' Will said, like a child learning a lesson by rote.

'So this morning there's no cooking, just eating,' she continued, keeping her voice light, knowing that their truce, this new lighter mood, could be swept aside with one wrong word. But she breathed a little easier, smiled a little more as he stayed with her rather than retreating. She finally broke their eye contact and reached for the teapot, wanting something to do with her hands to help her resist the foolish urge to reach out and touch him.

'So I just have to eat? You didn't trust me with a knife this time?'

The smile spread from Maya's lips to her eyes at Will's attempt at a joke. From white knuckles to this was quite an achievement, though the slight tension in his shoulders told her he was still a long way from comfortable.

'I'm not letting you get off quite that easy,' Maya replied, and then took a deep breath.

This was a risk, but there was no point them working together, no point them trying, if all they could do was speak pleasantries. They had to be able to use this bond she could feel forming between them to get the job done, get Will thinking, *feeling* about food.

'We're going to eat and talk.' Maya could have sworn she saw him pale at the thought. This was the reaction she'd expected to fish guts, not to talking about tea and cakes. 'We'll start with something easy. I promise.'

She tried to think tactics while she poured the tea. Should she push when he was so uncomfortable? She knew already that there was more to Will's aversion to food than she had first realised, that there was a painful connection she could only guess at. But he was the one who had asked her to do this, to help him appreciate food. He had asked to come; he had asked to stay. She could be sensitive, but she wasn't going to give up.

She passed him the bowl of raspberries. 'Try one of these.'

Will took one of the berries, stuck it into his mouth and swallowed it whole.

Maya rolled her eyes, laughing. 'Why don't you try that again? And give yourself a chance to taste it this time.'

Will did as he was told, and held her gaze seriously as he took another berry from the bowl and chewed slowly, deliberately, before swallowing.

'How did it taste?'

'Nice.'

He said the word confidently, and she guessed he wasn't being deliberately exasperating. He just didn't let himself feel anything more than that. He'd had so much practice at blocking it all out that 'nice' seemed like a perfectly reasonable answer. Well, it wasn't, and he had to know it.

'You said you were going to *try*,' she reminded him. 'From now on the word "nice" has been excised from your vocabulary. I want you to *think*.

I want to learn the flavours and textures you like. I want you to learn those things too. Neither of us can do that if everything is *nice*.' She waited for a response, but the silence between them grew heavier. She was the first to crack. 'You said you were going to try,' she said again, more gently this time.

She wouldn't cave, she decided, fighting against every instinct that told her to help him. Because all her efforts, all her tiptoeing and pushing and careful planning, would mean nothing if he wasn't prepared to commit to this. If he wanted to sit in silence—fine. If he wanted to get up and leave— fine. But she would not be the first to speak. She leaned back in her chair, crossing her arms across her body and fixing Will with a stare, willing him to try, to give her a chance.

'Sour.'

So much time had passed she'd almost forgotten why they were sitting there, but at the sound of his voice a smile spread across her face.

'Perfect!' she declared, as if this were the most insightful comment ever to be made about a raspberry. Well, she was willing to bet it was the most insightful thing Will had ever said about a raspberry—or any other food for that matter. And it was more than that, it was proof he was trying. 'And the texture…?'

She didn't have to wait this time.

'Soft,' he said, his voice quiet and even.

'Great.' Her arms spread wide in delight and her smile spread further as she spooned some cream onto a shortbread biscuit and sprinkled some of the chopped berries on top.

'Try this.' She wanted to tempt him with something delicious, something that would make 'nice' impossible. He was doing so well, she was finally getting through to him, and she didn't want him to lose this momentum.

He took the biscuit from her and bit into it. She could see the cogs working in his brain as he tried to think of something to say. She tried sitting there, watching him struggle—his eyebrows drawn together, one hand rubbing at the back of his neck—but she longed to step in. Now he had got started, and looked willing to learn, a few pointers and a little help seemed only fair.

'So…' she started, leaning towards him, giving him a chance to come up with something. Anything.

'The biscuit was sweet,' he said decisively. 'Crunchy.'

She thrilled inside at this first evidence that they were winning. She didn't even know what it was that they were fighting, but that didn't make it any less of a victory. He was finally giving her a chance to show him the pleasure that could be found in food—in her food, in *her*. She lifted a hand to her forehead at that thought and shook it away. *That's not what this is about,* she told herself. *This is about Will.*

About helping him—because he'd asked her; because he needed it.

'And with the raspberry?' she prompted, keen for him to pursue his line of thought and build on the bond she could feel strengthening between them. The trust that was implicit in his simple statement.

He took another bite of the biscuit, chewed slowly, and then caught a drop of cream from his lower lip. Maya caught her breath. Her attraction to him had been simmering away in the background, but the swipe of his tongue on his lower lip brought it to a steady boil. She leaned back in her chair, hoping that the extra inches of space between them would cool her off, get her mind back on the food, where it should be.

She watched him as he swallowed, closed his eyes, apparently deep in thought. He leant forward as he opened his eyes and spoke precise, considered words.

'I like the contrast.'

He liked the contrast. He *liked* the *contrast*. He had eaten her food, thought about the different tastes, and then expressed how the food had made him feel. This was hope. Light at the end of the tunnel. She'd been so hurt by his rejection of her food, of *her*, that this reversal stole her breath and her control. Perhaps her growing feelings for him weren't something to hide from. Perhaps they were something to nurture, to explore. If he was opening up about food, then what else in his heart was changing?

'That's brilliant,' she said, leaning closer.

A grin had spread over Maya's face and Will couldn't help reciprocating. *This shouldn't be so hard,* he told himself, enjoying the sight of the smile spreading across peachy pink lips and bright green eyes sparkling with encouragement. But

what she was asking of him was even more difficult than he had imagined. He'd known that being
in a kitchen with all the memories of happy times
he could never recover would be painful. But he
hadn't imagined that his every sense would be assaulted. That a scent could summon a memory,
that a taste would bring him pain, a texture remind
him of all his losses. And he couldn't flinch away
from them. Not if he wanted to succeed.

It felt as if every word this morning was another
step along a tightrope. If he was to fall, and Maya
pulled out of their deal, then his job would be gone
and the Julia House project along with it—and that
wasn't an option. He wished they'd not given the
hospice her name. He might not be here if they
hadn't. But failing the project was failing *her*, and
after everything she had done for him he didn't
want to let her down.

But Maya was making life hard. She wasn't
doing it on purpose. She couldn't know why
something so simple was so difficult for him—
couldn't know that for him thinking about food
meant thinking about Sunday dinners around a
scrubbed oak table in a steamy, fragrant kitchen. It
meant thinking about illicit fish finger sandwiches

with Julia before Neil, his foster father, got home from work, and it meant thinking about a creamy, sticky gateau with thirteen candles.

If he let go now, lost his focus even just a little, he knew he would never again find the calm that he'd spent years perfecting. Maya was asking him to open his senses, to enjoy food, enjoy life, and it seemed such a reasonable thing for her to expect. But impossible for him to deliver.

He reached for another of the shortbread biscuits and took a bite. Maya looked at him again, expectant, waiting. He wanted to be able to do this. Wanted her to see that he was trying, taking this seriously. He needed her to see that if he was going to get her to stick to their deal. And—much as he didn't want to think about why—he liked it when she smiled. It seemed as if the expression jumped from her face to his, as if her happiness spread from her body to his. Every time it happened he longed to do it again. He tried to force the feeling away, to box it up somewhere safe, somewhere he wouldn't have to think about it. Feelings like that—feelings that might one day lead to affection, to desire, to love—brought pain.

'Describe the biscuit,' she said, breaking into

his thoughts, as if it was the simplest thing in the world. 'Give me the first word that comes into your head.'

Just one simple word. His elbows were leaning on the table, and this thought dropped his forehead into his hand. Breaking eye contact, breaking *any* contact. He closed his eyes against the torrent of memories. *Home.* The last place that he remembered eating freshly baked shortbread. Not his expensive apartment, with its view of the city skyline, but a modest semi in the suburbs. That was the only place he had ever called home, and he couldn't go back.

'Don't let yourself think about it,' she said.

Maybe she thought he had nothing to say. Maybe she thought that he was scrabbling for ideas, not for sanity.

'Just say whatever pops into your head.'

He glanced up and met her eyes. Was she doing this on purpose? Had she found a weakness and decided to pick away at it? But her smile, though faltering now, when he looked up at her, showed no guile. She thought she was helping. She was just doing what he'd asked of her after all.

But Julia had baked that first day he'd gone

home with them, and he couldn't fight away the memory of it. He'd installed himself at the kitchen table, with earphones in and his maths homework in front of him, hiding in plain sight. Julia hadn't tried to talk to him, to coax him out of his self-imposed isolation. She'd just got on with what she was doing. And when she'd placed the plate of still-warm cookies on the table and pulled out the seat beside him he'd taken out his earphones and smiled cautiously.

'Don't tell me if you like it,' Maya persisted, her voice encouraging. 'Don't tell me if it's good or bad. Just tell me something about the biscuit.'

'Is there a point to this, Maya?' he asked, crossing his arms over his body, knowing that his tone was harsh, that he was being cruel. But he couldn't take this any more.

There was only so much pain he could bear, only so many memories he could keep at bay. Around Maya it felt as if he was constantly at saturation point. As if her colours and her joy and her enthusiasm took so much energy to fend off that he had no reserves to fight off the memories too. It wasn't her fault—she wasn't doing it consciously—but the effect was the same. He hated the look on

Maya's face as he spoke—a guilt-producing blend of shock, disappointment, pain. But he'd had to do *something*. Maya's gentle words threatened to undo fifteen years of determined effort, and he couldn't let that happen.

'Because it doesn't seem like we're doing anything useful here. All you're asking me to do is describe a biscuit. It's not like it's rocket science.'

'No,' Maya replied, sitting back in her seat and crossing her arms to match his.

The shock had faded from her features and now she looked hard, angry. With good reason, he knew.

'It's *not* rocket science. A few weeks ago I couldn't imagine a grown man unable to offer such simple observations. But then I strolled into your office and you lowered my expectations considerably.'

The words tumbled from Maya's mouth, and he couldn't help but be impressed by this display of grit even as he regretted the hurt that he knew powered it. But as he managed to distance himself from the emotions that had caused his outburst, the implications of what he'd done started to filter into his brain. If she kicked him out, refused to cater the fundraiser, his career would be in serious trouble and so would Julia House. He needed to backtrack—and fast.

'I'm sorry,' he said, keeping his arms tight to his body, his voice level, trying to keep a tight hold on his emotions. He couldn't afford another outburst, another wrong word. 'I shouldn't have said that.'

From the angry set of her shoulders and the hurt etched on her face he knew his apology hadn't been enough. Dread churned his belly as he realised that he had to go further. That if she was to forgive him, if he wanted to keep his job and the charity afloat, then he had to explain his behaviour properly.

'Maya, talking about stuff like this. I find it... hard.'

'No kidding it's hard.'

Neither her voice nor her body language had softened. She kept her arms crossed tight across her front, and her eyebrows were drawn into a hard, distressed line.

'I feel like I'm banging my head against a brick wall. The minute I think we're making some progress you go and say something like that and I wonder why we're both here. You said you were going to take this seriously, and—stupidly—I believed you. What are you even doing here, Will? You have no interest in learning. You don't think that anything I'm doing here is important.'

Will shook his head, trying to think, to plan. 'It's not that. I know it's important to you. But I can't...' His voice trailed off, and when he looked up pain and disappointment were so clear on her face that he knew he'd gone way too far. He'd crossed a line, insulted her and her work. It was clear from the joy that she radiated when she talked about her food how much feeling she invested in it.

His words had cut her deep. If an apology wouldn't set things right, he knew that there was one thing that would—but it would cost him more than anything else to give it to her. The only chance he had was to tell her the truth.

He rubbed his hand against the back of his neck, taking a moment to try and compose himself, to try and think about how he was going to get through this, how he'd get the words out without revealing his vulnerability. Eventually he looked up and started speaking.

'When I was a kid,' he started, trying to distance himself from his words, trying to pretend it was someone else's painful life he was describing, 'I used to spend a lot of time in the kitchen with Julia, my foster mother, and being here—well, it's bringing back a lot of memories. Ones I'd rather forget.'

Maya opened her mouth to speak and the hardness in her face started to shift, falling into compassion. He took a moment to wonder at her—that she could so easily set aside her own hurts at the sight of someone else's pain. Then he stiffened, thinking that she was about to reach out to him. But perhaps she saw the movement, or guessed what he was thinking, and she stayed back, giving him the space he needed.

'Will, I—'

The chime of the doorbell broke her words, and Will felt tension leach from his muscles as he realised he had been granted a reprieve…a few moments alone.

Maya rose from the table and, after a quick glance back at him, walked away.

CHAPTER FOUR

WHEN MAYA HAD seen the look of relief on Will's face she'd been grateful for the interruption. It seemed that a few moments alone was what he needed, and she was also selfishly grateful to have been saved from having to think of an appropriate response.

As she opened the door she wondered whether they had imagined the bell—wishful thinking, perhaps—but then she looked down and saw a head of angelic golden curls.

'Carys, what are you doing here? Where's your mum?'

The three-year-old reached up for a cuddle, and as Maya lifted her she saw her mother appear from behind the people-carrier parked in the lane, holding hands with Dylan, Carys's four-year-old brother.

'Maya, I'm sorry to just throw them on your doorstep like this,' said Gwen, her neighbour, 'but there's a total emergency at the office and they need me to come in. I was wondering if there was any chance you could watch the kids for a couple of hours?'

Maya hesitated for a second. She wanted to help; the lines on Gwen's forehead told her that her neighbour really needed her, and Maya felt a shiver of dread at the thought of having to turn someone away who needed her help.

But she had promised to help Will first, and springing someone else's kids on him wasn't exactly fair. Perhaps she could help Will *and* Gwen—and not risk censure from either of them. If Will would give it a chance then perhaps having the kids around would help. Keep their minds busy until they could think and speak a little more clearly. Will had looked grateful enough for the interruption a moment ago: maybe he'd welcome its extension.

'Just give me a minute,' she told Gwen. 'I really want to help but I have a client taking a course this week. If he doesn't mind then of course the kids can join us.'

She bit at a nail as she walked out to the terrace, unsure what would greet her there. Will was sitting staring out over the fields, his brow slightly furrowed.

'Will?' He jumped as she spoke his name, and his gaze whipped to her face.

'Problem?' he asked.

'No, not exactly.' She squared her shoulders and forced her voice to be level. 'My neighbour's got a bit of a crisis and wants me to watch her kids. I can take care of them without it affecting the course, but I just wanted to check if it's okay with you.'

'You've said yes?' His tone was a little sharp, and she could see wariness in his eyes.

'Not yet. But she's really stuck and I want to help her.'

'Why?'

His question, his softer tone, and the genuine curiosity on his face threw her.

'Why...?'

He just nodded, watching her carefully. Her body heated under his gaze and she felt aware of her every movement. The rise and fall of her chest against the neckline of her dress...the slight breeze catching her hair.

'I want to,' she said. He waited for her to continue, and the question niggled at her. She'd never even considered that she *wouldn't* want to help. 'The normal reasons, I suppose. Being a good neighbour, a good friend. Helping someone who needs it.'

He nodded slowly, but his scrutiny didn't let up.

'Okay,' he said eventually, slowly, as if he were already regretting it. 'Fine.'

She walked back to the hallway, unable to shake the feeling that she'd just misstepped somehow— as if Will had seen something she hadn't wanted him to. But when she spotted Carys and Dylan her face broke into a smile. Carys reached up her arms and Maya hitched her onto her hip, turning to talk to Gwen.

'All sorted. I'd love to have them,' Maya said. 'Do they need lunch?'

'Oh, that would be great. They've not eaten. I can't believe I didn't think about that. Are you sure you don't mind?' Gwen asked, though she was already walking back through the front door. 'Thanks, Maya, you're such a star. I promise I'll be as quick as I can.'

Maya wished she had a camera when she walked out onto the terrace with a toddler on one hip and a child clinging to her other hand. Will was standing by the table, his hands planted firmly in his pockets and his face grave. *He looks like he's heading for the electric chair*, Maya thought, suddenly doubting the wisdom of this move. This might push him too far, ensure that the whole endeavour was ruined. He stood there silently, not moving, and Dylan took another half-step behind her, his hand digging into the flesh of her thigh for security.

'Carys, Dylan—can you say hello to Mr Thomas?' She tried to make her voice cheery and welcoming, hoping it would break the stand-off between Will and the kids, but neither seemed fooled by it.

She widened her eyes at Will, pleading with him to make an effort. He could have just said no. He'd agreed to the kids being here—he couldn't carry on like this. With her gaze fixed on his, she realised he wasn't being difficult or rude. Not on purpose, anyway. It was as if he'd been frozen. His lips were even slightly parted, as if he'd meant to speak.

She ached to help him, could feel fear and pain radiating from his body. But she'd heard Gwen's car disappear down the lane so they were all stuck with each other for the time being.

'Will?' she said gently, not sure if he would even be able to hear her wherever his mind had taken him. 'If you want to go back inside...back upstairs?'

It was as if her voice had brought him back, snapped him into the present, and he pulled his hands from his pockets. One went to rub the back of his neck and Maya breathed a sigh of relief.

'No. I'll stay,' he said with grim determination. 'Hi, Dylan. Hi, Carys.'

Maya could just about hear the responses mumbled into her hair and hip. She'd never seen the children so shy before, and knew that they must be picking up on the tension between her and Will.

She'd resolved in the hallway to try and put Will's harsh words behind them. They had hurt. The direct insult had hit her where she was most vulnerable, and she wasn't sorry that she'd lashed out and stood her ground, that she'd shown him that she wasn't prepared to let him make her feel like that. The honesty and openness he'd shown when he'd told her the truth weren't a free pass. It didn't mean he could get away with speaking to her like that again. But it was the surest sign she'd had that this was working. That she and her food were getting through to him. And she didn't want to lose that progress.

When the afternoon was over they'd both have a decision to make: where was their relationship, such as it was, to go from here? Will needed to come to terms with the fact that if he wanted the course to work it was going to get emotional. And she had to learn his boundaries—when to push, when to give him space. If they couldn't do that, then he'd have to go.

'Now, I don't know about you three,' she said, trying to be bright, 'but I'm hungry. Who wants pizza?'

She didn't get the rapturous response that she'd been hoping for, but at least Dylan came out from hiding behind her skirts. She bustled the children back into the kitchen and set about finding aprons for them. Will walked through too, carrying their plates from earlier, and stood watching as Maya tied aprons, rolled sleeves and washed hands.

She left the children drying their hands by the sink and went over to him.

'Thanks for agreeing to this,' Maya said. 'And

for sticking with us. The lesson won't be exactly as planned but I'll keep to it as closely as I can.'

'No problem,' he said.

The emotion that had leaked into his voice stilled her, and she dropped the tea towel she was using to dry her hands. He was standing close, just a foot or so away, and she looked up at him. He looked sincere, and for a second she said nothing, did nothing. She couldn't break her gaze away from his, and he didn't look away either. The urge to reach out to him almost overwhelmed her, but she knew it would spook him, knew it wasn't what he wanted. She wasn't sure it was what she wanted either. He'd proved today how easily he could hurt her.

She nodded. 'Let's forget about it for now. Are you okay with these two for a second?' she asked, knowing that she was pushing her luck but hustling off to the pantry.

With the door closed, she leant back against one of the shelves and took a deep breath, trying to slow her heartbeat before she went back outside.

She didn't know quite what to make of Will's revelations. It wasn't her he was fighting, it was his past, his memories. She should feel pleased, but knowing everything that stood between Will and happiness made him feel further away. He'd opened up, but he'd hurt her too, and her feelings for him had never been so conflicted. How could she imagine that anything might happen with a man who could cut her so effortlessly? But how could she ever walk away from the bond she felt strengthening with every conversation?

Finally, feeling somewhat calmer, she grabbed the pizza bases and toppings she'd prepped earlier and shuffled her way back into the kitchen. Will greeted her with a look of relief. Once she'd separated the squabbling children and installed them on high stools Maya started handing out the ingredients and ladling sauce into the middle of each pizza. She was grateful for the noise, the chaos, the distraction, and watched, amused, as Will observed Dylan and Carys attacking the pizzas with zeal. She'd made pizza with them once before—it wasn't the first time Gwen had dropped them off in a hurry—and they'd both started spreading the sauce around the base. Carys with a spoon and Dylan, somewhat unconventionally, with his hands.

Maya spoke across Dylan's head. 'I hope this is

okay? It is what I'd planned for us, but not exactly under these circumstances.'

'It's fine, but—pizza? It doesn't really feel like cooking. I didn't even make the base.'

'It's about the ingredients,' Maya explained, glancing at the bowls on the counter, all of which appeared to have acquired tomatoey handprints. 'I thought we could try a few different things, talk about the different flavours...'

Her voice trailed off as she realised what she'd said. She didn't want to push him further—not just now. She looked up and found his gaze on her, his expression thoughtful.

Did he feel it too?

A connection flared between them. Something holding them together even when they both fought hard against it. She'd caught him looking at her, and she couldn't help but wonder if he liked what he saw. And then there were moments when everything stilled, when she saw, heard, felt only him. Heat crept up her cheeks as she remembered how he'd pulled her close after bandaging her finger, how much she'd wanted him.

A red slimy hand slapping onto her arm snapped her back to the present.

'I've finished!' Dylan shouted.

Maya forced her thoughts about Will away, hoping she'd been able to keep them from her face, and looked down at the three pizzas on the counter. Two were loaded with sauce and cheese and toppings. The one at the end had just a perfect circle of rich red sauce.

'Dylan, Carys, why don't you tell Will which are your favourite toppings. I don't think he can decide which ones he wants best.' It seemed like a good idea, enrolling the children to help teach Will. She sensed that they'd pushed each other as far as they could today. Using the kids as her proxy would give them both a little space.

When Dylan and Carys declared the pizzas finished she slid them into the oven and started mopping up tomato sauce—the children had got it everywhere, including all over themselves. She handed a clean cloth to Will—the handprints up his arms and across the front of his T-shirt testified to the fact that Dylan had overcome his initial shyness.

Twenty minutes later Maya watched Will as she placed the pizzas in the middle of the table. They'd all agreed to share, and Will gamely reached for one of Dylan's slices, an unusual anchovy-egg-pineapple combination. She wondered if he knew how gross it was going to taste. Probably, she reasoned, but likely he just didn't care. He took a bite of the pizza and Maya couldn't help laughing at the look of disgust on his face—maybe they were getting somewhere after all. This morning they'd covered good flavour contrasts; this afternoon they'd covered bad.

Will saw that Dylan was watching him and faked a grin. 'Mmm, delicious,' he declared, taking another bite.

When the pizzas were finished, Maya's question, 'Who wants pudding?' was greeted with shrieks from the children.

Will helped Maya to carry the plates into the kitchen and tried to avoid tripping over Carys, who had followed them. Their fingers brushed as he passed her the stack of plates and Maya waited for him to flinch. Although he tensed he stayed close; it was she who pulled away. This was dangerous, she told herself. Indulging these feelings would lead to hurt and heartbreak. She almost wished they were arguing again; it made it so much easier to keep this attraction of hers at bay. *Get a grip,* she told herself as she turned away and concentrated on dessert.

She loaded up a couple of trays with the left-overs from elevenses and they carried them back out to the table.

'Okay…' Maya slipped back into teaching mode. The children were giving her the perfect excuse to keep things simple. 'We're all going to make the nicest biscuit or cake that we can with the ingredients on the table. Then we'll all try some of everything. How does that sound?'

She decided that there was no point shying away from the fact that Will had come here to learn, but she could keep the lesson gentle, knowing he didn't need pushing further after this morning.

Thankfully there was not much room for disaster here. She wondered how Will was going to handle this—would their difficult start to the day have had any impact? He reached for the short-bread and she worried that he was going to repeat what she'd made for him this morning. Repetition wasn't a bad way to learn, but it wouldn't exactly inspire confidence that he was making progress.

But he veered away from the shortbread and picked another biscuit instead. He took a spoon and tested some of the whipped cream, the spiced cream, a few of the different types of fruit. Without saying a word he took a spoonful of the spiced cream, spread it deliberately and evenly over the biscuit, and finished it off with neat rows of pineapple.

Will presented the biscuit to her and then leaned in close to the table, watching her face. He looked nervous and she felt a shock of excitement at the knowledge that he was making such an effort for her food, for *her*.

She picked the biscuit from the plate and took a bite. The tang and the sugar from the pineapple worked perfectly with the spiced cream, and the crack of the biscuit between her teeth contrasted beautifully with the smoothness. Delicious. Of course it could be a fluke, but she preferred to believe that maybe this was another baby step in the right direction. At this rate they might even make a proper, grown-up-sized step by the end of their week together. And where would that leave her? If he could do this, start to feel, rather than fight off his emotions, what did that mean for the spark between them?

'Are you okay with Dylan for a few minutes?'

Maya asked when they'd finished clearing up. 'I think Carys is ready for a nap.' And *she* was ready for a few minutes away from Will, she admitted to herself.

'What am I meant to do?' he asked, apprehension clear on his face.

'Just have some fun,' she said. Did it always have to be so hard? 'Read a book, I think there are some in the bag Gwen dropped off. Build a tower out of something, or play football in the garden. I'll only be ten minutes.'

She headed upstairs with Carys, drowsy on her shoulder; then tucked her into her bed and gave her blonde curls a stroke. As she watched the little girl fall asleep, enjoying the calm and quiet her mind could find when she was away from Will, shouts erupted from the garden. Maya hurried to the window, worried about Dylan, but when she looked down she saw that two of her plant pots had been requisitioned as goalposts, and that the noise was just part of Dylan's elaborate goal celebrations. She glanced towards the bed, making sure that Carys hadn't been disturbed, and then leant against the window frame, watching the boys playing in the garden.

Will was running with the ball, a grin on his face and his body loose and relaxed. He gave an exaggerated dummy, but then deliberately lost the ball to Dylan, who ran determinedly towards the goal. With only a metre or two to go, and Will fake running dad-style behind him, Dylan's foot landed on top of the ball and started to slip. Maya raced to the door, knowing that he was about to fall and wanting to get to the garden before the inevitable tears and bruises.

When she reached the hallway downstairs she realised she couldn't hear any shouts, any tears, and then panic really kicked in. With a hurt child, quiet was always bad.

Maya ran through the kitchen and out through the back door, full of dread. Red-faced and breathless, she reached the garden, but Dylan was running about without a mark on him. Will, on the other hand, sported an impressive grass stain down his left arm and his jeans and his elbow oozed blood.

'Is everything okay?' Maya gasped. 'I saw Dylan trip and—'

'Will caught me!' Dylan shouted. 'But then he fell over too.'

Will shrugged. 'It was nothing; we're fine. But we need a goalie. Are you game?' His voice was a little tentative, as if he was as unsure as she about where they stood with one another this afternoon.

She gave him a long, considered look, trying to assimilate this fun, fearless man playing games in the garden with the one who had snapped and snarled at her this morning. Impossible. But she saw his words as what she hoped they were: an olive branch.

'Go in goal, Maya!'

After another glance at Will she kicked off her sandals and took up position between the plant pots as the boys kicked the ball between them.

Will laughed at something Dylan said and she found herself fascinated by the carefree happiness on his face. She'd never seen him look like that before, and it threw into stark contrast the expression he usually wore. In it she saw the extent of his grief, the control he must constantly exert in order to keep his emotions at bay. A few hours ago she'd been ready to pack his bags for him and show him the door. But this glimpse of the man Will could be, if only he allowed himself to be happy, changed her mind.

* * *

'Thanks so much again, Maya,' Gwen said as she steered the children towards the door late that afternoon.

'It's no trouble,' Maya said, trying not to sound as weary as she felt.

It had been no trouble since she was a teenager, stepping in to help in a crisis. It was hard to say no, especially when someone just turned up on your doorstep with an emergency. Occasionally, when she was reorganising her day in order to accommodate an urgent favour that just couldn't wait, she wondered what it would be like to say no. But then why *shouldn't* she help her neighbours and friends? Certainly not just because of a little inconvenience.

Will walked up behind her as she was saying goodbye at the door and Gwen looked at him with obvious admiration. Maya blushed and rushed to introduce him. 'Gwen, this is Will Thomas—he's on the cookery course this week.'

Will reached past Maya to shake Gwen's hand, and stayed close, though he never let their bodies touch. Maya craved the feel of his solid bulk against her, but knew she mustn't lean in to him.

'Pleasure to meet you,' Gwen said. 'I'm so sorry; I didn't realise that Maya had a course this week. I hope the children didn't get in the way?'

'It's fine—we had fun,' Will reassured her.

Maya stayed at the door to wave at the children, who were shouting goodbye from the back of the car. She had to step back a little to close the door and for a fraction of a second Will's body pressed up against her. Maya held her breath, wondering when she was going to make herself move away. When he would move. But neither of them did. Not until she felt herself relax just a fraction.

Will stepped back from her and Maya looked out of the door one last time, desperate to hide the blush she was certain was rising on her cheeks. She was furious with herself, with him, and so very hurt. She hadn't *meant* to step into him like that—she'd just needed to get out the way of the door. But in that moment when they were touching she'd wondered what it might mean…if it meant anything at all. With one decisive step backwards Will had told her everything she needed to know—a banner couldn't have been clearer: *Not Interested. Off Limits. Back Off.*

'So, peace at last,' she said, trying to cover the

pain of his rejection with false cheer as she walked back to the kitchen and started tidying. 'You don't have to do that,' she said, when Will followed her into the room and started to help.

'It's fine. About this morning…'

The last thing Maya wanted was to rehash this morning's harsh words. They'd tried so hard to get back on track, and it had worked—right up until that moment at the door.

She held up a hand to stop him. 'Look, I think we both said things we didn't mean. I think that, if we can, we should just forget about it and try and move on. If you still want to stay, that is?'

'I do,' he said. 'And I will try. I *am* trying.'

'I'm glad.' She fell silent for a long moment; she *was* glad—whether that was a good idea or not. 'Right, I'd scheduled a couple of free hours before dinner, so feel free to go for a walk, or…' he was already reaching for his phone '…do some work. I'll meet you back here at six.'

'Sure.' The look of relief on his face at the prospect of a couple of hours away from her stung, but she stored the feeling away for when she needed a reminder of why developing feelings for Will was a seriously bad idea.

At six o'clock Maya walked back into the kitchen, not feeling quite as refreshed as she'd hoped. She'd planned to have a quick shower and change her clothes, but the menus she'd been developing for a garden party later in the month had absorbed her so much that time had slipped past unnoticed.

As she reached the kitchen door she realised how much she wanted to look her best around Will. Of course he might not notice—or care; that was why he was here, right? Because he didn't appreciate the sensory aspects of life. But surely he knew enough about women to know what he liked? Maybe it was better like this, she reasoned. Keeping him at bay with a crumpled skirt and frizzy hair. It seemed easier than trying to keep her own feelings in check.

When she walked through the door into the kitchen Will was ready and waiting, a chef's apron tied around his waist. He was still trying. She broke into a smile despite herself.

'So, Will, what do you do when you're not working?'

It was a brave conversational gambit, Maya acknowledged as she took a bite of pastry, given his usual reaction when she asked him to talk about himself. But small talk had to start somewhere. They couldn't eat *every* meal in silence.

'I work a lot,' he replied, looking a little uncomfortable but not yet running for the hills. 'It doesn't leave time for anything else.'

No mixed signals there, she thought, her mind drifting back to the moment when he had stepped away from her earlier. She stored the thought away again: protection against future weakness on her part.

'But what about you?' he added, skilfully turning the conversation away from himself—a trick Maya guessed he'd performed more than once. 'How long have you been running your business?'

'Me?' She knew that he was deflecting her questions, but she grinned anyway. Just the thought of the business that she'd built always had that effect on her. It delighted her, thinking of how many people she'd cooked for and taught over the past few years. And talking about her was still talking. An infinite improvement on last night. 'I've been going for four years now.'

'You've built quite a reputation in such a short

time,' Will said. 'And I know new catering businesses often struggle in the early years.'

He looked impressed, and she guessed that his business brain was busy calculating her turnover, gross profit and costs per head. He probably couldn't help but think of her business as an accumulation of figures. She almost felt insulted, but knew that wouldn't be rational. She couldn't change the way he saw the world—all she could do was try and make a little room in it for the things he wanted to learn. But perhaps by the end of the week he'd be able to see the parts of her business that she really loved—the relief on a client's face when she pulled off a perfect béarnaise sauce in thirty-degree heat, the sigh of pleasure when a customer took a bite of a duck breast cooked to the perfect shade of pink, the sparkle in someone's eyes when their runny poached egg oozed over delicately smoked salmon.

'And this place?' he asked, gesturing towards the cottage with his arm and looking—to Maya's delight—genuinely interested. 'Have you been here since you started?'

'No. I used to have a kitchen in London, to be close to my clients. But I bought this place because

I needed somewhere to get away from it all. I find London so…cold. So unfriendly. I wanted somewhere I could relax and feel part of a community.'

'And how's that working out for you? Babysitting aside?'

She looked up to find his gaze on her, an astute look in his eye. She couldn't shake the feeling that he was criticising her, even though she couldn't exactly figure out why.

'I like it.' She spoke slowly, treading carefully. 'It makes such a difference, living somewhere you can get to know people. Big cities are so anonymous. So lonely.'

'So many people to meet,' Will countered.

'I prefer it here. The sense of community. It's…'

'Familiar?' Will suggested.

Maya shook her head, as if dislodging a troubling thought. 'What's wrong with that?'

'Nothing, I suppose. I think I'd miss the variety, though. In a city there's always someone new to meet.'

Always someone new to disappoint, Maya thought. Another person to try and please, wondering the whole time if she'd figured them out right. No, it was better here, where she knew her neighbours, knew her community, and clients found her through word of mouth.

'Maybe you should try it more often?' Maya suggested. 'Taking a break in the country.'

She watched the start of a smile form at the corners of Will's mouth, saw the fine lines around his eyes that told her it was starting to spread. And then as quickly as it had begun it was gone. Replaced by a look of complete professional calm.

'I don't think that'll be possible,' he said. 'So, have you always cooked?' Once again he steered conversation away from himself.

'No,' Maya said, trying to decide whether she was more disappointed or relieved that Will hadn't taken her words as an invitation to come and stay with her again. She hadn't meant them that way. The words had just slipped out before she'd had a chance to think about the damage they might do. 'The kitchen was always my mother's domain at home.'

'And you didn't cook together?' His blank face held for a beat and then, for a brief moment, Maya saw the shadow of profound pain cross his features.

'No. I would have just been in the way.' She

tried, but she couldn't keep the sadness out of her voice. She'd been so close to that chill in recent days, to the iciness that only memories of her parents could bring. She'd spent the last ten years trying to banish it, to force it from her life by creating colour and happiness wherever she could, but it seemed that tonight it was determined to follow her.

'So what made you decide to set up your business?' Will asked.

She imagined he had spotted her distress and thought he was steering the conversation back onto safer ground. But she couldn't let him run like that. Eventually he was going to have to face some of those emotions he seemed so scared of. You couldn't divide life into business and feelings, and she couldn't disconnect her business from the money that had started it. She shouldn't—couldn't—expect him to face his pain and not do the same, encourage him to stay while running away herself.

'My parents gave me the money to start the business. It arrived one day out of the blue and it was enough for my culinary training and to start the business I'd been thinking about.'

Will looked uncomfortable—no doubt because the conversation had taken another turn into the personal. 'I'm sure they're very proud,' he said, almost as if by rote.

Maya gave an involuntary snort at the thought of her parents being proud of anything she'd done. The look on Will's face told her it hadn't gone unnoticed.

'You're not close to your parents?' he asked.

Maya let out a long sigh. 'I've only seen them a handful of times in the last decade,' she said. 'They live abroad—the Caribbean, the last time I heard. They send money occasionally, but that's all they do.' The heaviness in her chest seemed to drag at her shoulders, closing her in on herself. 'I wanted so much to make them proud, but they aren't. It doesn't matter what I do, how hard I work.'

She fought against the pressure in her chest, pushing her shoulders back, painting on a smile, determined not to let her parents spoil this evening. But they'd both dropped into a thoughtful silence.

'Anyway,' Maya declared eventually, determined the night wouldn't continue in that sombre mood, 'enough about that. Do you want to check on dessert or shall I?'

Will gave a small sigh—of relief, she guessed—and even managed a smile.

He disappeared into the kitchen with their empty plates in his hands and a grim expression on his face. Maya listened as the oven door opened and then closed, glad to have a few moments to gather her thoughts. She never spoke to anyone about her parents, and the wrench she'd felt at her heart as she recounted their sad relationship had made her realise how hard Will must be finding his time here. She felt a stab of sympathy.

Will returned a couple of minutes later with two bowls of perfectly golden pie and steaming custard. Maya breathed out a sigh of relief. She'd have eaten it whatever it looked like, but this was even better than she'd hoped for.

'Okay?' Will asked as he placed the bowls on the table.

'Perfect.'

The rest of the evening passed pleasantly enough, and the easiness that was creeping into their conversation helped her shake off the memory of her parents' rejection. But it was strange,

Maya thought as she got ready for bed later than night, that she still knew so little about this man who was sharing her house. Even though they'd talked all through dinner, he was still a stranger to her.

CHAPTER FIVE

'A FARMERS' MARKET. That sounds great. And we're going there because…?'

Maya smiled. Fake and forced his enthusiasm might be, but at least Will was trying. She'd been prepared for terse Will this morning, after she'd heard him tapping away on his laptop after she'd gone upstairs last night, and again when she'd headed down this morning, but despite the black bags under his eyes he was making an effort.

Even exhausted he looked delicious, she thought, trying not to lick her lips. A little ruffled, not quite the composed, serene man she was used to. He looked altogether more human, and harder to resist.

'No one reason in particular.' She reached for the coffee pot to distract herself and poured them both a second cup. 'Let's just go, try and enjoy it, and see at the end of the day what we both got out of it.'

'But it's a market,' Will persisted.

Maya could see him trying to understand.

'So we'll be buying food—is that not the point?'

Maya took a sip of coffee and started a slow, deliberate count to ten.

'We have more than enough food for the week already, actually. I want you to try and go into this without any preconceptions. A shopping trip doesn't *have* to be about filling the cupboards.'

He nodded slowly, and Maya was worried by the look of intense concentration on his face. He was overthinking this already, and they hadn't even left the house. But she told herself to stay positive. They'd had plenty of setbacks, but Will was making progress, learning. She looked up again from her coffee, and found Will watching her intently. A blush rose to her cheeks, but she couldn't make herself look away.

For days now she felt as if she'd been running from this, but sitting here, sharing breakfast with this man, suddenly felt overwhelmingly intimate.

She knew all too well the effect that one's company could have on your mood. Her lonely childhood had led to a miserable adolescence, and she knew now, but hadn't been able to see then, that unhappiness bred unhappiness. It was only after the magical day when she'd cooked that first meal for her university housemates that she'd realised that a smile was contagious too.

So she fixed hers back in place: today she would project nothing but delight. Even if it killed her.

Her mind wandered as they drank their coffee and she found herself wondering what Will must think of her. He'd made it abundantly clear that he didn't understand her, that he had never come across anyone like her before. But did he *like* her? That first day in his office his eyes had swept her, up and down. No doubt he'd been comparing her to the glossy women who worked for him. She'd spied them through the glass walls and partitions and met the perfect example in Rachel, Will's elegant assistant.

But since then there had been those moments when she'd felt his eyes following her as she moved about the kitchen, or he would look startled when she turned to him, as if he had been caught doing something he shouldn't.

And now, with his eyes on her face as they shared breakfast for two, she considered that he might like what he saw. She panicked. How could she not panic when faced with those eyes—grey, the colour of a winter sky, but somehow not as cold, not as hard as they had once seemed? One of them should speak. One of them had to break this silence. Her mug slipped from her fingers and shattered on the cool, tiled floor of the terrace. She hadn't realised her grip on it had loosened to such an extent.

She dropped to her knees and started gathering pieces of the mug—until the sudden appearance of Will's hand on her wrist stopped her dead.

'Let me,' he said in a conspiratorial tone. 'Your hands have suffered enough.'

He took a piece of china from her and Maya sat back on her heels, still too stunned to do anything useful. She shook her head, trying to dislodge the cloudy feeling that her shared look with Will had caused, and went to find the dustpan and brush. Perhaps it was just a strange manifestation of cabin fever, she told herself. But she was frightened of what that look might mean. It had been easy to write off her developing feelings for him, not allowing herself to indulge her crush when she knew that a relationship would be impossible. But what if that was changing? What if he *was* capable of more? She would never know what might happen without showing him how she felt, but if he knew and knocked her back she wasn't sure she could bear the rejection.

Will barely hid a snigger when he saw her battered old four-wheel drive, painted a joyful shade of magenta, and she half expected him to insist on driving his car—even though, from the look of the paintwork, this was the first time his sports car had been outside the M25. But he said nothing and climbed into the front seat without a word of protest. She smiled at this lack of pride.

As they stepped out of the car at the farmers' market she saw Will take in the scene and carefully watched his face for a reaction. Some slight tension around the eyes showed her that he was feeling uneasy, but he was here, and at the moment that was all that mattered. She, on the other hand, could not stop herself from beaming, taking a deep breath, trying to catch the smells of the stalls nearest to her.

To her surprise, Will's face broke into the hint of a smile. She'd seen his smile so rarely she'd almost forgotten how it transformed his face and lit up his eyes; it felt like a gift—another delicacy to add to the ones she knew were waiting for her on the market stalls.

'You look happy to be here,' he commented, and she was thrilled that his voice sounded light, untroubled.

'How can I not be? I know what's in store for us once we get started.'

'And what's that?' He looked suspicious.

'Well, I don't know about you, but I'm thinking cheese, fruit, bread—maybe some cured meat. That'll be lunch sorted. And then cake.' At the sight of apprehension creeping into Will's face she reached out and brushed her hand against his arm. 'Don't look so worried.'

As she withdrew she could hear the thudding of her heartbeat in her ears, and wondered whether she'd given herself away, made her attraction too obvious. But he didn't seem to have noticed. Instead the corners of his mouth lifted in a small grin.

'This market is like a theme park for you,' he said. 'You look like Dylan did yesterday when you brought out the pudding.'

'I can't help it,' she said, laughing, relieved that

he'd not read anything into her gesture. 'I mean, just *smell* it. It's incredible.'

Her jaw dropped slightly in surprise when he laughed along with her.

'So,' Maya said, 'do you want to stick together or separate?' She guessed that being surrounded by food like this might be a little intense for him, that he might want some space while he eased into it.

'Let's stick together,' he said, and she felt a warm glow starting to spread in her chest. 'I can learn more that way,' he added, and she crashed back down to earth. *Right.* He was here to learn—that was all. Because he wanted something from her, not because he wanted *her*.

They drifted from stall to stall, tasting and snacking, and Maya had never been more aware of another person's presence. When they stopped she had to school her hips to prevent them from leaning into him. Had to consciously stop herself trying to breathe in his scent. When her hand brushed against his as they were both reaching for the same cracker to sample a rich, spicy chutney, she let out a small gasp and had to feign a fierce competitiveness for the last unbroken cracker to hide her spontaneous reaction. She couldn't show him how she felt, couldn't even hint at it, because if he were to know and to reject her again it might just break her.

'Have you been to a market like this before?' Maya asked as they wandered on, making small talk, trying to distract herself.

A sudden look of pain on Will's face warned her that she'd wandered into dangerous territory. *Again*. Maya floundered. She hated herself for a moment for causing him anguish, but knew that such moments were necessary—were part of what Will had asked her for. It seemed every time she tried to speak to him she managed to hit a nerve, touch on some subject that brought those shutters behind his eyes crashing down.

'Once.'

And they were back to monosyllables. 'Did you enjoy it?' She couldn't keep tiptoeing around these questions. Will had asked her to teach him to appreciate food, and these questions, this pain she was causing him, were all part of it. To her surprise he stopped walking and looked at her intently.

'Yes,' he said eventually, slowly. 'I'd completely forgotten. I went with my family when I was thirteen...fourteen. Just before—' He stopped. 'I ate so much cheese I was nearly sick.' The distress on his face was replaced with a melancholy smile. 'I've not thought about that day for years.'

She had to force down a smile. She knew how sad he seemed, but this revelation was another little sign of their progress, that her teaching was working.

They turned and strolled on, and Will gave her another small smile as they came upon a stall selling cheese.

'Should I ration you?' Maya joked as he tried a couple of the samples, keeping her hands well away from him this time.

'Julia tried, but I didn't listen. She had no sympathy when I felt ill.'

'I don't blame her. She sounds like a sensible sort of woman.' She kept her voice light, tried not to show how thrilled she was that he was talking about his past, about food, about himself.

'She was,' Will replied, still smiling. 'But Neil was a soft touch. He brought me tea and toast and let me watch telly all afternoon.' Will's face fell then, and he turned purposefully away.

More pain there, she thought. More that she didn't understand.

'What's next on your list?' he asked, his voice harder, almost terse.

Maya blinked, taken aback by this sudden change in mood. 'I'm heading for the bakery.'

'Right. I'll meet you there,' Will replied. 'I left my phone in the car. Can I have your keys to go get it?'

She handed them over, and with that he stalked away towards the car park. She stood and watched him go, feeling an ache in her chest at how easily he could walk away, how easily he rejected her company.

'So who's your date?'

Maya turned at the abrupt question to find Gwen behind her.

'Oh, no. That's Will,' Maya reminded her, pulling herself together. 'He's on my course—he was at the cottage, remember?'

Gwen nodded, but her eyes were still following Will as he walked towards the car.

'Hmm… The way he keeps looking over here at you, I'm not sure I believe that.'

'Really?' The question sneaked out before Maya could stop it. 'He keeps looking over?'

'See for yourself.'

Maya risked a quick glance over her shoulder and found Gwen was right. Will was looking back at her. She gave a small sigh, because what if he *was* attracted to her? She'd lived the best part of twenty years with people who were cold and un-available, and they had made her miserable. And no two words better described the man who had pitched up on her doorstep on Sunday. There was no man on earth attractive enough to make her want to repeat the experience.

But she'd seen Will change over the past few days, seen a light at the end of the tunnel that sug-gested that his frostiness wasn't permanent. But without that to hide behind she was frightened. Because if Will was open to a relationship the question changed. It wasn't whether he wanted a relationship; it was whether he wanted *her*.

'So he likes you—and I'm guessing from the colour of your cheeks that you like him too. What's stopping you both?'

'Gwen.' Maya tried to speak firmly, know-ing that she had to stop this train of thought in Gwen's mind as well as her own. 'There's absolutely nothing going on with Will. How are the kids?'

'Oh, they're fine. Actually, the kids are the reason I came over to talk to you. You remember it's Dylan's birthday party this weekend? Well, I was so sure that I had everything sorted, and I thought I had ordered the fairy cakes, but I've just been to see Elaine—you know, from the bakery—and she says I never placed the order. She has a wedding this weekend and no time to do them. I'm a complete dud in the kitchen and I wondered if there was any chance that you—?'

Gwen was getting a little frantic, her voice rising and her hands gesticulating more and more widely. Maya reached out to catch one of her hands; she hated to see anyone upset, especially when she was able to help. She knew the question was coming, and even though she had no idea how she was going to manage it she knew that she was going to say yes. What else could she do? If she wanted to keep Gwen as a friend she'd have to find a way to do this for her.

'Of course I can bake some cakes, Gwen, if that's what you're asking.'

'Oh, Maya, thank you so much. The kids love

your baking and I know that they'll be so pleased. You're a life-saver. I don't know what we'd all do without you.'

Maya didn't let her smile drop until Gwen had breezed away towards the car park and tried not to think about what whipping up a hundred iced fairy cakes would do to her schedule. It was already tight, with prep and planning to do for the private functions booked in next week, and Will's dinner to prepare for if he got through the course. But what was she meant to do—say no? She cringed at the thought.

'Anything the matter?'

Will appeared behind her, wearing a calmer expression than when he'd walked away. Maya suppressed a sigh of disappointment. Once again when he was faced with something he didn't want to think about, something he didn't want to feel, instead of sharing it with her he'd taken himself off and come back smoothed over and closed off.

'Nothing,' Maya said, her mind returning to her schedule, still trying to work out how to rearrange it to fit the baking in.

'Dylan and Carys's mum—did she upset you?'

He sounded genuinely concerned, she thought,

and the touch of his hand on her arm shocked her into looking up at him. How did he do this? Going to automaton and back, constantly cycling. It was dizzying, trying to keep up, never knowing which Will she was going to get.

'I'm not upset,' she said, wondering at the way sensation seemed to spread from his fingertips throughout her body in swirling streams of warmth.

'Then why did you look so serious?' he asked, and his words snapped her back to the present.

She looked down at where he touched her arm and was surprised when her skin looked normal. She had half expected to be able to see ripples and waves dancing like light on her skin.

'She just wants me to make the fairy cakes for Dylan's birthday on Saturday.' There was no hiding the breathiness in her voice and she wondered if Will would notice it, if he would understand it.

He looked surprised. 'Surely you can't have time for that? You told me what your schedule's like at the moment. I take it you said no.'

'Oh, well, I hate to say no if I can help.'

'You said no to me.'

His words surprised her, and she looked up into

his eyes. He'd said the words softly, quietly, without heat or anger, but she sensed hurt behind them.

'That was different.' Because he'd already hurt her so much by then what had she had to lose? She couldn't have felt any lower than the moment he'd refused to try her food; refused to give it—*her*—a chance.

He looked at her for a long moment before he spoke, seeming to absorb her words. 'Right.'

She felt his scrutiny in her mind, her character.

'And this happens a lot, I'm guessing? Crises. Emergencies. Cakes. Babysitting. And you never say no?'

She crossed her arms, uncomfortable with the turn this conversation had taken. Of course she didn't say no. Why would she want to be lonely her whole life? Accommodating emergencies, helping people out when they needed it—it was worth it to have friends in her life. People who cared about her. And this week was about him, not her, anyway. She didn't need to be judged.

'It's nothing, Will. I just help out my friends if I can.'

But that wasn't enough—not for him, it seemed—because he took a half-step closer to her, kept his gaze on her face as he ran his hand through his hair and rested it at the nape of his neck. 'She's taking advantage,' he said.

Of course she wasn't. She just needed some help. Maya wondered what had Will so riled up. 'It won't impact on the course, if that's what you're worried ab—'

'It's you I'm worried about.'

He stepped forward again, his hands reaching for hers, but this time Maya took a step back, shocked at the strength of feeling in his voice.

'I'm just trying to be a good friend.' But his words had shaken her, and her voice wobbled as she tried to understand what he'd said, as she thought back over her friendship with Gwen, looking for evidence she could use to refute him.

He dropped his hands and crossed his arms after she flinched away. 'This isn't about her at all. It's about you. About you wanting to please her—please everyone. Is she a good friend to you?' he asked, stepping closer again. 'Or does she take advantage because she knows you can't say no?'

Maya raced through memories, looking for something, anything she could throw at him to prove him wrong. Gwen wasn't taking advantage, was she? Maya had never thought of it that way, never questioned whether there was anything wrong with a neighbour asking a favour. She assumed any of her friends would do the same for her if she asked. It was just that she never had—never wanted to be a nuisance, to put people out.

'It's not like that,' she said, but her voice was small, full of the doubt she was feeling. Why would he turn her doing something nice into something bad? Why did he even care? 'Don't try to make it sound as if she's doing something wrong.'

'I'm not saying *she's* doing anything wrong.' His voice was low and vaguely threatening. 'I'm saying *you* are.'

'That's ridiculous.' She bristled at his words, his accusation, and threw her hands in the air. 'How can you possibly twist it like that?'

'I don't think what you're doing is the problem, Maya. I think the reason you're doing it is. So prove me wrong. Why is it so impossible to say no? Why are you so desperate to keep your neighbour happy?'

My parents— She shut down the thought before it could fully take form. How could her making cakes be about her parents? Other than the odd

Christmas card and a couple of cheques, she'd not spoken to them in years. She barely thought about them. And yet she'd never stopped trying to impress them, trying to make them love her.

Will's calm expression belied the raw, ripping pain his questioning had caused.

'That's enough.' She spat out the words as she plucked the car keys from his hand and turned towards the car park. She ignored him calling after her. Tears pricked behind her eyes and she fought to keep them there, to stop them running down her cheeks. Tears wouldn't solve anything, she knew. The only thing that kept the sadness away was acting relentlessly happy. It was what she had to do, what she'd been doing for years to chase away the shadows of her childhood—and Will had seen straight through it.

Will stood in the middle of the market and watched Maya walk away from him. Torn between chasing after her and giving her space, he just stood for a few moments, struggling with indecision. The twist of guilt in his stomach reminded him that he'd taken things way too far. There was no hiding from the pain that he'd seen in Maya's face, and the knowledge that he'd done that to her—again—was devastating.

He hadn't set out to criticise her, to hurt her. He'd been genuinely worried when he'd seen how anxious Gwen had left her and had wanted to make her see that she didn't have to do this—didn't have to say yes every time someone asked a favour. But as he'd been speaking he'd started to realise where he fitted into this pattern too. She wasn't bothered about teaching him anything; she just couldn't bear that he hadn't liked her food and was determined to change his mind.

He thought back to the look on her face that day he'd first met her, when he hadn't given her food his full attention. Back then he hadn't known her well enough to recognise how hurt she'd been that he hadn't liked her food—or hadn't said that he did. But he could see now how much other people's opinions mattered to her. And not the way it did with the people he normally came into contact with, who either wanted the approval of their boss or a newspaper column.

When Maya felt the disapproval or disappointment of others it caused her real pain. He flinched at the thought of it. There was no point trying to please people all the time. He had discovered that long ago. Through a series of foster parents and children's homes he had learned that it didn't matter how well he behaved, how charming he tried to be—it didn't matter whether the people he lived with loved him or not—because he always got hurt.

And it wasn't even as if she had to *try* to please him. Just the sight of her, the smell of her, brought a smile to his face whether he wanted it or not.

But even if he'd judged her right, guilt over the way he had spoken to her gnawed at his gut, and he set off towards the car at a slow walk. He knew that the pain his memories of the market had thrown up had coloured his words. That he'd been striking out against Julia and Neil as much as he had against Maya. He breathed a sigh of relief when he saw the bright pink vehicle still parked where they had left it. He knocked on the window and Maya lifted her face from her hands and opened the door.

'I'm sorry. That was out of line.'

Maya nodded slowly.

Will climbed in the passenger seat before she

could change her mind, and then turned to look at her, not knowing what sort of welcome to expect.

'Out of line,' she mumbled, 'but maybe a little true.'

He'd wanted to help, pointing out that she didn't have to constantly try to accommodate everyone, that a friendship should go two ways, but it had backfired, and he'd hurt her. He felt a strange ache in his arms, and knew the only thing that would cure it would be to pull her to him, try and soothe the pain that he'd caused. But he couldn't do it—because where might it lead? It could never be just one touch, he knew. The passion that he'd felt the few times their skin had brushed told him how much he had to fear from her. That if he ever got her in his arms he'd never want to let go. And that was too big a risk.

He opened his mouth to speak but she shook her head slowly, thoughtfully. 'Not now, Will. Let's just get home.'

They arrived back at the cottage and Maya went straight to the kitchen with the few bags of food they'd bought. Will followed behind at a distance. He knew that he should leave, that he'd said too much, felt too much already, but he didn't want to.

And somehow the fear he felt of confronting his memories was rivalled by the fear that Maya might make him go and he would never see her again.

He gave a small shudder. He had sworn fifteen years ago that he would never let anyone close enough that losing them would hurt, but somehow over the past days Maya had crept beneath his defences.

He tried to imagine the life he would be going back to—his dull, grey, cold life. And he realised that all the things that had terrified him when he'd met her, and that still terrified him—her passion, her joy, her colour—he couldn't imagine life without any more. He didn't want his life as it had been before her. Yet he couldn't risk contemplating a life *with* her.

Eventually she returned from the pantry and found him leaning against the counter.

'So what now?' she asked.

'I'm sorry,' he said again. 'I shouldn't have said what I did.' His eyes fell on the kettle. 'Should I make some tea?'

Maya laughed—a brittle chuckle that sounded as if it had travelled through tears. Tea? It did seem a little ridiculous. But it was what Julia would have done, and he didn't know what else to suggest.

'So…tea? Is that what Julia would have recommended?'

He knew that her use of his foster mother's name was a challenge. If he wanted to stay they couldn't keep dodging this—he couldn't keep dodging *her*. Eventually they'd have to talk. And he was the one who had led them here; he'd decided to get personal. He'd brought up *her* parents. She didn't seem to want to talk about them any more than he wanted to talk about his. But if they were going to see this week through then he had to stop running.

'Probably,' he said. 'She thought there was little that couldn't be fixed with a pot of tea.'

'Like I said, she sounds like a sensible woman.' Maya took a deep breath. 'Tell me about her.'

At every mention of Julia Will's heart gave an involuntary clench. He fought hard against the feeling, pushed it out of his chest as he had learned to at the age of fifteen, had been practising ever since. But what could he do other than what Maya asked? If he didn't she'd ask him to go, give up on him. And if he went back to the office without her on board it would be a disaster for his career *and*

Julia House. At least he tried to convince himself that that was the reason why he was about to do this—why he was sorting through words and memories to find the best place to start his story. That this was why he was so desperate to stay, couldn't contemplate walking away from her yet.

'I was in care from when I was a toddler.'

He sat down at the table as he started speaking and nudged the handles of the mugs and teapot with his fingers, focusing on them, not brave enough yet to look up and meet Maya's gaze. But then she reached across the table and her fingertips brushed against his. He wondered if it was an accident, if she was aiming for the teapot, but then her fingers twined with his and she gave his hand a gentle squeeze.

'I've never known the full reasons why I was taken in by Social Services, but a family couldn't be found to adopt me and I lived the next few years in group homes. I guess the longer I was there, living without a real family, the harder it was to find someone who would take me. When I was about twelve Julia and her husband, Neil, visited the home. They were registering as foster parents and wanted to meet some of the children who might be placed with them. I don't know what Julia saw in me...'

When Maya laced her fingers with his a little tighter, brushed her thumb across his, he almost drowned in the sensations it provoked. Her touch offered support, courage, sympathy, strength. Finally he looked up and met her gaze. In her face he saw nothing of their angry words, no trace of the hurt that he'd inflicted on her. Her eyes were sad, but somehow he knew that it was *his* sadness that was reflected there. She had encouraged him from the moment they met to open up, to engage with her, to show her what he was feeling. And now that he was doing it she didn't shy away. Instead she anchored him with her fingers and listened.

'I didn't go out of my way to be friendly to Julia. By that time all I could think about was keeping my head down and counting down the hours till I could leave the home, leave school, get on with being independent. She came over and chatted to me, and I thought nothing much of it. A few months later I was told they'd like to foster me.'

He took a breath and squeezed Maya's hand, borrowing some of her strength. He knew that he had to lay out all the faults and insecurities and fears that had led to his hurtful words, and just hope that Maya could forgive him.

'I wish I knew what it was about them that made me give it another shot. Maybe I could see it was my last chance to have a family. I was with them for two years before Julia started to get sick. It had taken a long time for us to start to feel like a family, but eventually—somehow—it started to work. There were kick-abouts in the park with Neil, and helping Julia in the kitchen. Sunday lunches and trips to the shops—all the everyday stuff that had baffled me for years.'

When the Wilsons had taken him in he had thought that was it. He had finally found somewhere he could be loved, be safe. He had even dared to start loving them back.

And that had been his biggest mistake.

'When she first got sick none of us realised how bad it was going to get. They'd caught it early, they said, the lump, and so her prognosis was good. In the end it just meant a long, drawn-out year of suffering—for her, for all of us.'

First he had watched as his foster mother had grown thinner and paler. He'd held her hand when her hair fell out. And then, after he had said goodbye to her for the last time, he'd realised his foster father was gone as well—to a dark, lonely, scary place where there was no room for a foster son. So it had been back to the group home.

On the day he'd returned Will had decided two things. One: his memories could do nothing but hurt him, so he would lock them away. Two: he would never let anyone he loved leave him again. And the only way to guarantee that was never to love.

The first of those promises was well and truly broken now, and he couldn't see any way to fix it. But the second…? Maybe he could still salvage that one. He needed to find some limits again, keep Maya at a safe distance. Once he knew that he could see out the week, that she would cater the fundraiser, he would never have to see her again.

'Will, I'm so sorry,' Maya said, and he could see from the tears brimming in her eyes that she was feeling every moment of his pain as he was. 'So your foster dad…' she said eventually. 'Neil?'

'Neil's another story,' Will said, wanting this to be over now, hoping that he'd explained enough for her to forgive him. 'Can we leave it for another time? Today's been—'

'A lot. I understand.'

'So, did you have anything planned for us this afternoon?' Will asked, briskly untangling his fingers from hers and locking them tightly around a mug. Even the burning heat of the porcelain couldn't mask how empty his hand felt without Maya's palm safely enclosed.

'Er…we were meant to be baking.'

She looked flustered, as if she hadn't realised that she'd reached out for him until he'd broken the connection. He forced himself not to notice the blush that rose on her cheeks.

'Baking's fine.'

'I thought we could try a few different breads,' she said, and he nodded at her vaguely. 'I had a few ideas when we were at the market that I'd love to try out.'

'Fine.' He gripped the mug harder and spotted the way her gaze lingered on his knuckles. She couldn't have failed to notice the shift in the atmosphere, but he refused to dwell on it. This was what he had to do to survive.

She talked him through different types of bread, her voice faltering and unsure, her gaze sneaking sideways at him when she thought he wouldn't notice. He pushed her further and further away from him in his mind with every word. And, as he'd known it would, his world grew duller and colder. But he knew how to live with this bleakness. If he didn't do this now—didn't protect himself—if he fell for her, he wouldn't survive in that world.

By the time he had all his ingredients formed into a smooth dough he thought that he might have found some sort of equilibrium.

'Now you can pretty much pummel it,' Maya announced.

Her blunt words had him snapping up his head to look her in the eye. She'd watched his retreat, he gathered, and was fighting back.

'You need to knead the dough, but I don't mind how you do it. Fold it, roll it, stretch it, throw it on the counter. It's up to you.'

That he could do. He methodically folded and then pressed the dough with the heel of his hand, exactly as she was, and with each movement he shut out the world a little more until there was nothing left of his memories or the pain. No room for Maya in his new mantra: *Fold, press, turn. Fold, press, turn.*

Eventually, she spoke.

'Will, that'll do.' Her words were sharp, terse.
He wouldn't care.

He looked up at her. 'We're done?'

'We're done. It just needs to go somewhere to prove.'

They were done. That was all he needed to know.

'Will!' she called, just before he disappeared up the stairs, her voice full of trepidation. 'Don't forget we're booked in at the pub for dinner.'

Dinner tonight. There had been something in the paperwork she'd sent over about this. Something to do with palette and identifying flavours and supporting local businesses too. It was an integral part of her week-long cookery course. He sat down on the bed and leaned forward, his elbows resting on his knees. He didn't know if he could do this. It had taken ten minutes of unbroken concentration and repetitive kneading to achieve any semblance of calm and peace.

And then, with one sentence, she'd undone all his solid, unrelenting effort.

He rubbed his forehead with the heel of one hand and reached for his phone with the other. Stroking the smooth glass with his thumb, he scrolled through his emails. He dashed off a couple of replies and then re-read the one from a Julia House board member, passing on Neil's contact details and telling Will that he'd love to be in touch again.

Will's thumb hovered over the 'delete' icon, as it had a dozen times in the past weeks, before he closed the message. He replied to a few more urgent business emails and waited for the familiar action to ease the tension from his shoulders and the ache from his insides. But relief did not come. Even after he'd fired up his laptop and spent an hour going through the Julia House financials he still couldn't shake Maya and the disappointment on her face before he'd come upstairs from his mind.

He stepped into the shower and turned on the taps. It was only when the icy water hit his shoulders that he realised he'd instinctively set the temperature to cold. Even that realisation caused an unwelcome flood of images. The light in Maya's face as she bit into a pastry; the way his skin had scorched when she'd laced her fingers through his, offering silent support; the delight in her eyes as he'd enjoyed her shortbread.

He stepped further under the water and allowed

it to pound on his head and drive out the flame of desire the memories had provoked. With his hand resting against the tiles he leant into the spray, letting the heavy stream of water beat at the tension in his muscles. He washed quickly, letting every drop of cold water draw the emotions of the day from him. He would not leave the shower until he could think of the look of hurt on Maya's face without it hurting him. Not until he was sure he could think of her dispassionately. And only when his neck and shoulders felt numb from the cold did he allow himself to turn off the taps and reach for his towel.

He pulled on his charcoal suit and a black shirt and smoothed his hair. When he looked in the mirror he was satisfied with the result. There was nothing on his face to show his struggle. To test his defences, he allowed an image of Maya entry to his mind. Her face that day when he'd answered emails rather than eat her salad. His shoulders tensed, and he had to push hard on the door that kept his guilt out—but it did shut. This was going to be okay, he told himself. He could get through this. But he was under no illusion that tonight was going to be easy. Maya didn't batter her way through his defences; she smiled and laughed and charmed and listened until he threw open the doors and invited her in. He had to be more careful.

CHAPTER SIX

As MAYA WAITED in the kitchen for the sound of Will's steps on the stairs she shifted the waistband of her dress—a bright flowery tea number—and wondered if there was time for her to change. The dress was one of her favourites, and she'd thought that tonight she'd need the cheering effect of the turquoise flowers and the full fifties-style skirt. But now it felt like too much. She had watched Will mentally retreat this afternoon, leaving her with a bland automaton, and somehow turquoise, pink and orange didn't seem quite appropriate any more.

She always took her students to the local pub; it was good to see whether they could identify flavours and techniques, and sample a style of cooking other than her own. It was normally a lively, boisterous evening, with plenty of good food, good wine and good conversation. Well, two of those should be manageable—as long as there wasn't some sort of crisis at the pub—but the last seemed almost impossible. After what had seemed like a major breakthrough earlier, when Will had told her about his childhood, his later silence had seemed like a quid pro quo.

Will fixed his eyes on the dessert menu, determined not to look up until he had found something resembling control. He'd been searching for it all through the meal, but every time he'd thought he had it, every time he'd thought she was safely shut out, he saw something, smelt something, tasted something that brought everything crashing back. When they'd been back at the cottage getting through this evening had seemed simple, if not necessarily easy. All he had to do was keep a safe distance between himself and Maya; shut her out in exactly the same way he'd shut everyone else out over the past fifteen years. It was the only way to stop himself from falling.

'What are you thinking? Dessert?'

And there was the problem. Every time he thought he'd found control she found another way back in, and it didn't seem to him as if she was even trying. It wasn't as if she was pushing, or looking for his weak spots. It was just something about her, the way she overwhelmed all his senses, that made her impossible to ignore.

This time it was a simple question about dessert; last time it had been the sight of pink nail varnish against fiery red hair; the time before that the way the soft cotton of her skirt had brushed against his leg when she'd turned suddenly.

He lowered his menu and looked up to see her watching him. Frustration was etched into her features.

'Fine, if that's what you want,' he replied, keeping his voice carefully neutral.

Her sigh, not quite as supressed as he guessed it was meant to be, cracked his control a little further. He looked up at her again—and wished he hadn't. She was leaning forward on her elbows, examining the menu, and the button at the gently curving neckline of her dress strained and then escaped.

When looking away didn't work he took a long sip of his red wine, hoping it might bring him some measure of calm. But the taste, the flavour, was so *voluptuous* it kept his mind in the one place he shouldn't, *couldn't* allow it to rest.

It was so tempting just to give in. To open his eyes wide and drink in the sight of her, to stop fighting it and let her gravity pull him in. But what happened when he crashed to the ground? He wouldn't endure another loss—had no intention of rebuilding his life again. This time when Maya asked the question he kept his eyes determinedly neck up. They rested on the plump curve of her bottom lip.

No help at all.

'Chocolate pudding,' he declared, surprising himself. Because that was just what this situation needed: rich, gooey, decadent chocolate pudding.

When Maya's tongue darted out to moisten her lip he knew he had to do something drastic.

He drew his mind away from Maya, away from the pub, away from his thoughts. Concentrating all his effort on protecting himself, he ran through columns of numbers in his head. Mentally scrolled through the spreadsheets sitting on his laptop. He calculated gross profits, net profits, tax liabilities and risk exposures. And when he let himself back into the room he could look at Maya without needing to reach across and touch her. Success—for now.

He glanced down at the chocolate pudding—he hadn't even noticed it arrive—with trepidation.

Maya let go of a sigh of relief as the waiter placed her dessert in front of her. She was so tempted just to give up. To tell Will to leave, that she would cater his dinner—anything to end this torturous week. But every time she thought back to everything he had told her, to the way he had gripped her hand when he'd spilled the secrets of his past, she knew that she had come too far to walk away from him now. She just had to get through this cheesecake and then she could go home. No more half-finished sentences, no more monosyllabic answers, no more staring at the tablecloth rather than meeting her eye. She could get home, get out of this dress and go to sleep. A few hours' hiatus from the heartbreak of seeing him give up.

To test her guess as much as anything, she asked, 'How's the chocolate pudding?'

'Fine.'

She flinched. But then held out her spoon, half wondering if she was mad to do it. 'May I?' she asked.

She was about to reach across when Will's

spoon, laden with chocolate pudding, appeared in front of her nose. He caught her eye at last and held her gaze in a challenge. She didn't back down. Still Will didn't look away.

The pudding was divine. Rich, moist, decadent. But—and she couldn't resist a small smile of satisfaction—still not as good as hers. She licked her lips, not wanting to waste any of the rich chocolate sauce, or the opportunity to get a reaction from Will. This was the closest he'd felt to her since they'd finished their tea and tackled bread-making earlier. A few hours ago she'd watched stone-cold Will shut the other Will—the one with the beating heart and human emotions—out. She had even seen the physical change as his shoulders and jaw had tensed and his eyes had become unfocussed, as if he were looking through her, not *at* her.

It had hurt so much, knowing that it was deliberate. He'd let her in, let her close, and then regretted it. Had forced himself back out into the cold and left her alone. It had cracked her heart, knowing that even with the bond that had been forged between them over tea and secrets he could walk away from her so easily.

But right now, in this second, he was definitely

here. His eyes drifted up from her lips to meet her gaze.

Desire was written plainly in his eyes, clear and unguarded. The knowledge went straight to her belly and then dropped lower, heating, awakening. She couldn't forget all the times that he'd hurt her in the past few days, but she couldn't hide from the intensity of his expression either. Couldn't hide from the fact that he was fighting demons—and perhaps could only win if she stuck with him. If she stuck around, put her heart on the line, she might get hurt. If she walked away without knowing, she definitely would.

And then—*bang*. The shutters slammed hard and she gasped, as if her fingers, her heart, her whole body had been caught by them and crushed. The only consolation she had to temper the pain was that it had seemed harder for him this time— almost as if the battle playing out in his mind was growing fiercer. But whether it was hard or not to shut her out it didn't matter. All she knew for sure was that he kept doing it.

Maya forked cheesecake into her mouth as she tried to soothe the pain in her chest. Perhaps she should take a leaf out of Will's book? She closed her eyes. She would take herself away from here, just for a moment, find some peace. She tried to guess the ingredients of the cake: the usual of course—ricotta, cream, vanilla, a hint of lemon—but there was something else there too. Something unexpected. She kept her eyes closed, not wanting anything from the outside world to distract her, wanting to focus her whole mind on this simple task.

'Maya?'

Her eyes flew open at the sound of his voice. And she cursed her body for its lack of caution.

'Where did you go?' he asked.

'Nowhere.' She didn't bother hiding the hurt from her voice. Why should she spare his feelings when he had no regard for hers? 'I'll get the bill.'

She breathed a sigh of relief as they walked back through the front door, thankful that this night was nearly over. Not even the sight of Will's gorgeous face across the table had made the dinner pleasant.

For some women she supposed it might be the cheekbones that made him so attractive, or the hint of muscles beneath his shirt. For her it was the fine lines that appeared during those rare moments when he smiled, the reminder that he was still human underneath, however hard he fought against it.

He'd barely spoken over dinner. Every time it had looked as if he might, every time she'd seen that light in his eye that told her that he was there, the moment had passed. But perhaps, after how close they had felt this afternoon, tonight was the wake-up call that she needed—a reminder of how disastrous getting involved with Will would be. Because she couldn't live her life waiting for those moments, looking for those lines, waiting for a hint of something more than cold tolerance.

She'd been there before—constantly trying to get some reaction from the people who were meant to love her—and she wouldn't do it again. She knew that she liked making people happy. With Will's input she was starting to see that she liked it a little too much. But that didn't mean she should be looking to spend time with someone she could never please.

'Well, goodnight,' Maya said at the bottom of the stairs.

'You're not coming up?' Will's words were gruff as he crossed his arms.

'No. I need to get back in the kitchen.' She'd

never spoken a truer statement. She needed her kitchen; she needed space. She needed distance from him and the pleasure that only her art could bring.

'You look tired,' Will blurted out, and Maya sensed he hadn't meant to say it.

She bit her lip. She wasn't going to let it get to her—wasn't going to let his words hurt her. She knew that he hadn't meant them to cut. He'd not given them—*her*—any thought at all. They'd just spilled from him on the spur of the moment.

And she didn't care that he thought she looked tired, she told herself. She did look tired. She *was* tired. But to have him stand there in his immaculate suit and shirt, with his perfect bone structure only improved by the hint of tomorrow's stubble, and remind her that she didn't quite match up hurt. It was further proof, if she needed it, that even if Will was interested in a relationship she'd be crazy to think he'd be looking for one with her.

'Well, great—thanks for that. I'll see you in the morning,' she said, turning and walking into the kitchen.

She heard the kitchen door open and knew that he'd followed her in. She wished he hadn't. Wished she could have some time to patch up the grazes she'd accumulated that evening from his glancing blows. And she didn't want him to see how much he had hurt her. Somehow that seemed like protection. If he saw her feelings for him then he would feel as if he had to say something. Let her know that he didn't return them. Showing him what she felt would be opening the door to rejection, and she didn't think she'd be able to stand that.

'Maya, I only wanted you to see—'

She whipped around and stared at him, stopping his words with a raised hand. What right did he have to make her try and see anything? He was the one who had her feeling like this: confused, overwhelmed, unsure of herself. With his constant advances and retreats, the unending shifts between them. And now he'd decided to *worry*?

She looked up and met his eyes, and his expression made her gasp. She had never seen him wear a look so intense. Not even when he was talking about his past. And she understood it instantly. Any chef recognised hunger when she saw it.

He took another step closer to her and she took half a one back, trying to preserve the space between them. Trying to protect her heart.

'It's okay, Will.' Her voice shook. She had suspected that he was attracted to her, had seen flashes of interest in his eyes, felt the chemistry between them. But nothing like this. Nothing so raw, so unguarded. 'I *am* tired, but there are a couple of things I need to do tonight.'

The words felt insubstantial, weightless compared to the energy thrumming between them, the intensity with which he held her gaze, the anger, hunger, fear that simmered in the air.

'You're only in here because of the extra job you took on. The cakes for the kids' party.'

That was what he wanted to talk about? Why he was looking at her as if she was a cold glass of water on a hot day? Why his voice had turned rough and low.

'Yes, and I need to get on. So, goodnight.' She couldn't take much more of this. One minute she was drawing small talk from him as if she was extracting a tooth; the next he was marching into her kitchen and picking a fight over her schedule. He'd changed his mood more times than she could count in the last few days…hours. How was she meant to keep up? How was she meant to know what *she* was feeling when one minute he was acting as if she wasn't even in the room and the next was looking at her as if she was everything he needed?

'It's late, you're tired, and you're about to pull an all-nighter because you're afraid of upsetting a neighbour. Why *is* that?'

What the hell did that have to do with anything?

At least it made it easier to know what she was feeling—anger. That was enough. Her face grew hot as she battled to keep her temper. She didn't know why he was pushing this, but it stopped now.

'It's none of your business, Will. I think you should go up.'

'But I think it is my business,' he said, raising his voice. 'Because why ever you're doing this is the same reason I'm here. The same reason you won't cook for someone who doesn't like your food. I'm not here to learn. I'm here so that you can convince me to like you.'

Tears rose behind her eyes, but she used her anger to fight them down. She would *not* let this man drive her to tears. His words were cruel, and felt more so because she knew that he was right. He had taken one look at her life and seen exactly what drove her. Exactly what caused her heart to ache every time she thought of her parents. Exactly what made her so desperate to make everyone around her love her.

But what else was she supposed to do? Go back to her life before, with no love, no affection, not even any warmth? She'd found a way to enrich her life, a way to be around people that made her happy. Was she supposed to turn her back on it because it involved a few late nights and reorganised days?

But part of what Will had said struck home. Perhaps this *wasn't* the way things were supposed to work. All one-way, giving all she had just to get a shaky friendship in return.

Will was wrong about one thing, though. 'You make it sound like I tricked you into this—like I forced you to be here.' She ground the words out through gritted teeth and a tense jaw, not wanting to get drawn into a discussion, wanting to be left alone. But she had to correct him if this was what he thought had led them here.

'You think I'm doing this out of choice?'

'That's exactly what I think,' she said, furious enough to forget her resolve and argue. 'I walked away and you came running after me. Don't turn this around.' She spat the words, flinging her arms wide for effect.

'I had *no* choice,' he said, his face showing his fight for control.

'Really? What was so important that you couldn't find someone else to cook? We both know you don't care what you eat, so why do this? Why put *me* through this?' Her voice had started to shake with the last words.

'Because Sir Cuthbert Appleby threatened my job and Julia House if I didn't. *That's* why.' His voice broke as he threw the words at her, one hand coming up to rub his forehead and his neck, as if the admission had been painful to expel.

Maya's hand flew to her mouth as she took a step backwards, reeling. *That* was why he had come? Because he'd been threatened? Nothing to do with her. Nothing to do with food or feelings, or anything that he had led her to believe. The shock curdled into hurt as the implications hit home. All this time she'd thought that it was his past that was keeping him from engaging with her. His memories that made him run. But it wasn't that at all. He just didn't want to be here. Didn't want *her*. He never had. Of *course* this was about money. She'd been kidding herself that he was in any way interested in learning anything.

'Maya, listen to me—'

'Just go!' she shouted across his angry words. She didn't want excuses, or even an apology. What she wanted from him had never been on offer. She'd had enough. Enough of his ups and downs, his steps forward and back. She'd watched him change direction so many times now her head was spinning. She just wanted quiet. Wanted her kitchen and her peace. 'I've had enough, Will.' She hoped that careful, reasoned words would make him go. 'I know being here is proving difficult for you, but that's not my fault. I never asked you to come.'

She turned her back to him and started washing her hands. Maybe he'd take the hint and leave her in peace.

'You didn't,' he said, his voice coming from close by her ear, so near that she could feel his warm breath on her skin. 'But I'm here.'

She jumped as two strong hands settled heavily on her waist, and she fought against her body's impulse to enjoy it, to beg for more. She longed for it. For his arms around her, his lips on hers.

But she couldn't shake her doubts. What would it do to her if he disappeared again?

'I don't know what this is, Maya,' Will said, turning her to face him.

She couldn't look up and meet his eyes. It would be too much, too intimate. She knew that if she did it she'd give in. But he lifted a hand to her face and cupped her jaw gently, tipping face up towards him. She closed her eyes.

'I don't understand it. If I had a choice I'm not sure I'd even want it. But you came along and—'

'I didn't do *anything*,' she said, opening her eyes, her flash of anger giving her the courage to face him down.

'You did something,' he said, his voice low, gravelly, outrageously sexy, his thumb stroking her jaw. His expression carried a hint of accusation. 'I don't know what, or how. But I never expected this. Never realised I'd have to fight so hard…'

His words tailed off as his gaze dropped to her lips. His desire was written in every line of his face. Her hands skimmed up his arms, still unsure whether to push away or pull closer, and with every one of her pounding heartbeats resisting grew harder.

If her lips met his there'd be no turning back. No more hiding from the desire that flickered between them,

His hands slid further round her waist, pulling her tight to him, and with one long sigh she knew that she was lost. She stretched up on her tiptoes and met him in a searing kiss.

She'd fought against this as hard as he had. It had been difficult enough when Will was being surly and taciturn. When he was pressing up against her, solid and hungry, his hands worshipping her, it was impossible. And yet as the shock of that first taste of his lips receded, rational thought fought its way back in. She moaned, thinking that she might never find pleasure like this again and knowing with absolute certainty it had to stop.

Will mistook her moan, though, for as it escaped her lips he backed her up against the kitchen counter, his hands gripping her waist, lifting her.

She had to act now, because if she waited another minute, another second, she knew she'd change her mind. She lifted her hands to his chest, allowed herself just the briefest, lightest of caresses before pushing him away.

They both stood for a moment, as unmoving as

statues, and the only sound was the rapid gasp of their breath. When Maya eventually looked up at him she bit her lip as relief and regret warred within her.

'I—' he started, but she didn't want to hear that. Didn't want to hear that he was sorry for their kiss—not even if she knew herself that it had been a terrible idea. Hearing him say it would tear at her heart.

'Let's…'

She started speaking without knowing what she was even thinking, never mind what she wanted to say. Surely they had said enough already? Nothing had changed. This wasn't magically going to be easy. There was no 'easy' where Will was concerned. There was too much to think about tonight. And she knew that there were only two words that could keep the rest of this evening from getting any more complicated.

'Goodnight, Will.'

Will leant back against the kitchen counter, heart racing, breath ragged, feeling desperately empty. What had just happened? He hadn't meant to touch her: he just hadn't been able to bear her turning away from him like that, upset. And then once he had brushed his fingers against her he hadn't been able to let go. Electricity had crackled between them; resisting had become impossible. He'd had to kiss her, had to pull her closer. Every thought he'd had in his mind, every memory, every fear, every doubt, had been chased away by her hands in his hair, her soft lips, her hot body. He'd been lost. All he'd known was what he'd wanted. Maya. More. Everything.

Their kiss had assaulted all of his senses, and part of him was desperate to follow her and kiss her again.

When she'd pushed him away it had been as if part of his body had been torn away with her.

But now he was starting to remember all the reasons it shouldn't happen again; one kiss had his head rushing and his heart dangerously un-protected.

Instinct told him to run. The last few days with Maya had caused him more pain than he had expe-rienced since he was a teenager. But she'd brought him more delight too. That one brief kiss had been packed with more pure pleasure than he could re-member feeling before.

Slowly, he uncurled his fingers from the edge of the worktop. He had to fight this—as she was. He had to get these feelings back under control and be practical. Whatever his feelings for Maya, he had to consider Julia House too.

He hadn't wanted to get involved with the project initially, but one of the nurses involved in the project had helped to care for Julia and had seen Will's picture in the *Financial Times*. She'd persuaded him to become a trustee on the board, and Sir Cuthbert had agreed that the company would provide pro bono financial advice. He would treat it like any other project, Will had reasoned, just another spreadsheet.

But he could no longer think of Julia House as columns and rows and cells. Because he was constantly being reminded of those last weeks of Julia's life and of the people who had cared for her. Surely that care had a value that couldn't be entered on a spreadsheet? Which was why the thought of Sir Cuthbert pulling the project from him was terrifying. It wasn't just money or business on the line here; it was people's lives, their families, their memories. And after these last few days with Maya it had never been clearer how important those things could be.

CHAPTER SEVEN

MAYA'S ALARM BLEEPED on the nightstand beside her and she reached a hand across to turn it off. Six o'clock. She'd not got to bed until the early hours and had spent the rest of the night tossing and turning, trying to decide what to do this morning. Would she ask Will to leave? She knew that she should. Last night had proved to her that she couldn't trust herself to make the right decisions in the heat of the moment. That the strength of her attraction could and would overpower any sense of reason if given just half a chance. She should tell him this morning. Tell him anything he wanted to hear just so long as he would leave. Because he had to leave some time, she knew. And better that she sent him away than waited for him to disappear.

Or perhaps she wouldn't have to ask, she thought with a jolt. Perhaps he'd come downstairs with his bag packed and be out of the door before breakfast. Her treacherous heart lurched at the thought.

Being with Will, even when it was terrible, was always exhilarating. She said things to him she wouldn't dream of saying to anyone else. She could speak to him without double-checking every word, without worrying whether he was going to judge her. The first time they'd met she'd been overwhelmed with hurt at his rejection. But what had come after—the honesty and straightforwardness—it was refreshing. She felt like herself in a way she hadn't for years.

So he was the one person in her life she felt she could be truly honest with. Could tell him to get lost if that was what she wanted. But she didn't want to. Not yet. Not with that kiss still burning in her mind.

She decided to go downstairs early, stake her place in the kitchen, be waiting for him when he emerged.

Downstairs, she turned the radio on and then walked into the store room in search of fruit and yoghurt for her breakfast. She had to do something; she hated the idea that he would walk in and catch her staring into space like a dolt, know that she was thinking about him. She turned the volume up a little higher—the music would stop her straining her ears, trying to hear if he'd come downstairs, or for the sound of his car on the driveway.

When she walked back into the kitchen to find him sitting at the table, fake nonchalantly leafing through a newspaper, she nearly dropped the bowls she was carrying. Bright summer sunshine played in his hair, and she couldn't help but remember the way it had felt under her fingers last night—how she'd run a fingertip over that spot, just there, where light gathered on his forehead. Before he even looked up she could feel the rush of blood to her face.

'Morning,' she said, her voice wavering.

'Good morning,' Will replied in false surprise.

Maya was gratified to see him fidgeting with the corner of the newspaper. She couldn't resist a smile at this proof that he was not immune to her after all. That, as much as he might sit and pretend normality, he remembered how he had lost himself with her last night. From the look of his tousled hair and the dark shadows under his eyes, she wasn't the only one who'd had trouble sleeping last night.

She picked up a bag of granola mix and carried everything to the table, still wondering as she did so what she should do—whether to make him leave. By the time she'd left her room this morning she'd made up her mind to tell him to go, but this doubt and indecision on his face, this vulnerability that mirrored her own, made her doubt herself. And just because they weren't talking about this kiss it didn't mean that the memory of it wasn't there in the room with them. It was almost physical, its presence was so strong, and it marked her every movement.

Will stood, a careful, controlled smile on his face, as she approached and he reached out to take one of the bowls. His hand brushed against her as she passed it to him and she looked up and caught his eye when she felt heat radiating through her skin. They both stood still, their eyes locked together. Attraction and hesitation fought within her breast, pushing her towards him and back in equal measure. Her body appeared still, belying the struggle she felt.

Maya searched his eyes, trying to judge which

Will she had with her this morning. She saw neither stone-cold barricades nor the hot, passionate temper she knew was hiding in there somewhere. She saw only doubt and confusion. She looked away, hoping it would stop this pull she felt towards him. But it was there; it was constantly there now. And she wondered for the first time whether it would *always* be there, humming in the air. Even if she sent him away, even if he went, would they ever be able to break this or would it haunt her for ever?

She sat down opposite Will and spooned yoghurt, fruit and granola into her bowl. When she looked up Will was watching her thoughtfully. She looked away quickly again, embarrassed. Were they just going to carry on as if nothing had happened? They only had two days left on the course. Perhaps they *could* just ignore it? Who was she kidding? She could no more ignore this feeling in her chest than she could give up cooking.

As she lowered her spoon a sudden bright spot in her vision made her freeze in panic. *Oh, no. Not now.* Her body couldn't do this to her now—not with Will in the house. Not today of all days. But the second bright light confirmed it, and the churning of her belly told her she couldn't waste time sitting here. Her migraines weren't pretty, and they definitely didn't require an audience. She knew she had a few minutes to get herself to the bathroom, and that once she'd finished throwing up she'd need a dark, quiet room until the headache gave up its hold on her.

She dropped her spoon and pushed to her feet.

'Maya? What's wrong?'

From the concern flickering at the corner of Will's eyes she knew she looked as bad as she felt.

Trying to get away from the table, she stumbled. Making a dignified exit really would have been so much easier if her eyes would just co-operate and focus. But she whacked her hip into the corner and squealed in pain, curling her body in on itself.

'Maya, tell me what's happening.'

Will came to stand beside her and his palm, huge and warm, rubbed her injured leg. His other hand came up to cup her jaw, as it had last night, and the memory brought fresh tears to her eyes. He smoothed her hair from her face and tucked it behind her ear, then tilted her face so she had no choice but to look at him. She groaned. Why, of all days, did this have to happen now?

Because she'd spent all night trying to convince herself that what she felt for Will could be forgotten, ignored, destroyed, instead of sleeping.

'It's nothing,' she told him. 'Just a migraine.' *Just* a migraine. A migraine that would have her with her head down the toilet just as soon as she could get there, and then feeling that her brain was being skewered by a red-hot poker for at least the rest of the morning and probably the afternoon. Just a migraine.

'What do you need?' Will asked, and even through her disturbed vision she could see the worry in his face.

'Nothing. Just to get upstairs. I can manage,' she said, her stomach roiling. 'But I can't see...'

She tried to push away from him, but his arm came around her waist and he propelled her towards the stairs. She half thought about pushing him away, assuring him she could manage on her own. But she needed to get upstairs *now*, and this way did seem quicker.

She directed him to her bedroom and, with her queasy stomach warning her she was on a deadline, let him guide her. By the time they made it to her en-suite bathroom he was practically carrying her.

She sat on the side of the bath and leant against the washbasin for balance.

'Thanks for that,' she said. 'But I'll be—'

She was interrupted by the first wave of sickness and dropped to her knees, reaching for the toilet. She groaned when she realised that Will was right behind her.

'I'll be fine.' She managed to get the words out this time, but still he stayed.

He stayed through the noise and the tears. When her nausea abated long enough for her to catch her breath he ran a flannel under the cold tap and then pressed it to her forehead. She leaned back against the bathroom wall, eyes closed, trying not to read too much into this. But she couldn't help it. She couldn't quite truly believe that he was here with her. She knew what it must be costing him… the price he must be paying in memories. With the kiss last night, and now this, she realised that she couldn't trust anything she'd thought about him before today.

'Will, you really don't need to stay.'

'Maya, I'm only going to say this one more time.

I'm not leaving you alone like this. I know you don't want to inconvenience me, because I know that's how your mind works, but let me help you.'

She risked opening her eyes for a second, but winced at the bright light. Will reached up for the pull cord and turned it off, leaving them in darkness.

I know how your mind works. The words repeated themselves in her head. He really did seem to. No one had ever been close enough to her to do that. No one had ever taken her at more than face value. No one else had seen the loneliness and the pain that fuelled everything she did. Every failed friendship and frustrated relationship. But he was here, helping her, out of choice. Not out of obligation—she'd given him every opportunity to bail, and she couldn't have been more of an inconvenience, and he was still here for her.

'Thank you,' she said eventually.

'It's nothing. What do you need?'

She couldn't remember ever hearing his voice like that: soft, gentle, caring. What did she need? Him…like this…for ever.

And failing that? She wrinkled her nose and took a second to think, to consider the state of her stomach. The poker had started its steady push into the left side of her brain.

'I need to go to bed.'

Will took the flannel from her forehead and ran it under the tap, and then, despite her feeble protests, washed away the tears and grime. He handed her a toothbrush and a glass of water, and then one solid muscled arm slipped beneath her knees and another snaked around her back.

'It's fine, Will. I can manage.'

He shushed her protest and carried her back through to the bedroom. Looping her arms tight around him, she turned her face into his shirt as the door opened and light streamed in. His neck hid her from the light, and his skin was warm and smooth, and it also smelt delicious. Not even a migraine could dull the pleasure of being so surrounded by him, and from the thud of his heart he was no more immune than she. He deposited her gently on the bed, untangling his arms from around her, and went to close the blinds and the curtains.

'Can I get you anything?' he asked again, coming to sit beside her.

She tried to be practical, sensible, and directed

him to the various medications she needed from her dresser drawer. But what she really wanted was his arms around her again.

A sharp stab of pain forced her eyes shut and she knew that only sleep could make this better now. But she resisted for a few seconds, not wanting to break this spell Will had cast, before fatigue finally dragged her under.

When she woke she took a second to assess the damage. The nausea was gone, and her head seemed fine—until it was hit by a screeching sound. It took a good few seconds of agony before she realised that the sound was coming from *outside* her brain. The smoke alarm.

She jumped from the bed and swayed slightly, which reminded her she needed to take things easy for the evening. But the screeching didn't let up.

'Don't get up! It's all under control!' Will shouted over the din—from the kitchen, by the sound of it.

Maya hesitated and the noise stopped. What was she meant to do, though? Just lie here all day? No, she had too much to do. What was he doing down there? she wondered as she threw on clean clothes and headed for the door. Realisation struck when she realised what the smell was, and she actually faltered on the stairs, not quite believing it.

As she pushed open the kitchen door Will was depositing a slice of charcoal into the bin and the kettle was whistling fiercely on the stove. She pulled it from the hob, and a second slice of charcoal from under the grill, as Will fought with the foot pedal on the bin.

'You didn't have to come down,' he said, distracted. 'You've had nothing to eat or drink all day, and I read...' He glanced over to his laptop, and she could see the NHS website still open in his browser.

'It's fine. I wanted to see if there was anything left of my kitchen.' She laughed quietly, testing its effect on her head. So far, so good. But she dropped into a chair at the table, not wanting to push too much too soon. Her feeble-feeling knees had *nothing* to do with the sight of Will Thomas making toast for her, she told herself, though she knew it was a lie. She could still feel the air humming with the imprint of last night's kiss, though it felt different...warmer, somehow...less threatening.

'I had it under control,' Will said, cutting into

her thoughts as he sliced another slab of bread from the loaf. 'I just turned my back for a second to get the kettle on, and then the alarm started.'

Maya went to stand beside him, testing herself in proximity to him. 'Honestly, it's fine. I've been asleep for hours. I needed to get up.'

And she could hardly expect him to wait on her hand and foot after everything he'd already done. Everything felt different this afternoon. She tried to kid herself that it was Will's effect on the kitchen that was making it so—crumbs and bread knives and tea-making everywhere—but it was more than that. *She* was different; *they* were different.

'You need to rest,' Will said gently, dropping the bread knife and turning to face her. He reached out and stilled her hand as she went to open the tea caddy.

'You don't have to run around after anyone today. Can't you let me do this?'

His voice was warm and gentle, no fear or tension in it, but it wasn't the drained, empty voice of last night either. It was full and plump, rounded with…with what? Happiness? Contentment, perhaps? With Will's fingertips still brushing against her arm it was hard to argue with him.

His other hand dropped to her waist and turned her slowly around. 'Go back to bed; I'll bring this up in a minute.' He brushed her hair away from her face before pushing her gently towards the door.

She could hardly believe that one person could alter so much in such a short time. But he had. There wasn't the panic of the man who had run, scared, if he thought she was getting close to him. Nor was there the unguarded passion of the man who had kissed her in her kitchen. The man in her kitchen today was solid and sweet. Considerate. Kind. But she knew that the painful memories from Will's past weren't going to be solved by a chocolate pudding and a kiss.

And solid and sweet was lovely—really—but thinking that the passion between them last night might have been replaced with something cosier was not a welcome thought either. Solid and sweet was generally at its best right after something a little hotter and stickier.

But then she was changing too. Before all this—before Will—she wouldn't have been able to sit and wait while someone made her food; she'd have been down there in the kitchen, insisting on doing it herself, terrified that being a nuisance would drive him away.

All last night she'd told herself that this couldn't work. That she would never kiss Will again because he wasn't capable of giving himself to the kind of relationship she wanted. But he had been here for her today. Yes, she'd seen shadows cross his eyes, had seen sadness in his face, but he was here. He hadn't run away—neither in body nor in spirit.

Maybe he *was* capable of more. But that didn't mean he wanted it. Or that he wanted *her*.

CHAPTER EIGHT

Maya yawned as she climbed back into bed and sank into the pillows, letting her eyes drift closed. Her body felt loose, limp, and she felt herself melting into the mattress, the light summer quilt lying softly on her skin. She'd opened the curtains now that her light sensitivity was gone, but was too sleepy to enjoy the view. Migraines sapped her strength, but she was used to managing on her own. She'd been doing it for so long that she'd never realised there was another way.

Will appeared in the doorway with a tray in his hands, and looked around for space to put it. There wasn't a lot to spare. Her room had been described as 'bijoux' by the estate agent, and even that was generous. It should have been a box room, really, but when she'd launched her cookery school she'd taken the smallest room for herself so she could offer the more generously proportioned ones to paying guests. She cleared a couple of magazines off her bedside table and Will plonked the tray there and then stood beside her, looking awkward.

'Oh,' Maya said, shifting over a little, making space on the bed. She looked up at him, suddenly shy. 'It's really the only space in here.' *It's just the offer of a seat*, she thought. *He can't read anything into that.* Harder still to see double meanings when she wasn't even sure if there were any. Did she want to invite him into her bed? Did she even know?

After another pounding beat of her heart Will sat a little stiffly beside her and then reached for the tray. When he turned back he presented her with builder's tea and burnt toast with a grin on his face that suggested he had prepared a feast.

She smiled at him in return. It might as well be a feast: it was probably the only thing she could manage to eat after this morning's events. The novelty of being cared for gave everything a rosy glow and an added shine. It was startlingly easy, she was realising, to accept his help. And he showed her every time he smiled that her needing him was bringing them closer, not driving him away.

Will sat beside her and watched as she bit into

the first slice. 'Are you not having anything?' she asked, fiddling with the handle of her teacup.

'I don't know if we can risk me making any more just yet.'

'I can make you something,' Maya said reflexively.

She was halfway out the bed when Will gently grabbed her hand; she realised what she was doing and hesitantly lay back down. His warm hand anchored her to the bed, soothing her insecurities, her fears. She didn't have to do this with Will. Didn't have to try all the time to deserve his company. He wanted her to just *be*. A warm glow started in her belly and spread through her chest until it lit up her face.

'At least have a slice of mine,' she said, feeling her way around this new world, not sure what to do if she wasn't doing everything herself. 'I'll let you make us both some more afterwards if it will make you happy.'

'Fine,' Will agreed with a smile and took one of the slices. He bit into the charred bread and pulled a face. 'This is horrible.' His face dropped into a grimace as he spoke. 'Why are you eating it?'

'No, it's fine,' Maya lied, stifling her laugh and

forcing down the rest of the slice when she saw Will's downcast expression. She took a large glug of tea, wincing slightly at the bitterness. 'Here,' she said when she realised he didn't have a drink either. 'Have some of this. It'll help.'

'Thanks.' He took the cup from her, letting his fingers brush against hers as he did so.

As he took a sip of the tea Maya was surprised by how that intimate gesture sent a spark of desire through her belly. She had thought that they might be able to avoid facing what had happened last night. Not for ever—maybe just for a few hours. A little time to catch their breath, just to enjoy one another, but maybe it couldn't be that simple.

'This view's incredible,' Will said, shifting himself further down the bed, stretching out long legs and looking out of the window.

Or maybe it could be that simple...just for now. Immediately beyond the cottage's garden a meadow of wildflowers stretched for nearly half a mile. And beyond that evening sunlight glinted on the river that meandered through the valley. She walked down there most days, thinking over recipes, breathing in the smell of the countryside, taking snapshots with her camera for future inspiration.

'It's beautiful,' Maya said with a grin on her face. 'I much prefer it here to my old London life. I could never have run my own residential cookery school in the city.'

'It *is* beautiful here,' Will agreed gently, carefully. 'And you should be proud of your business. But is this what you really want? Don't you feel you're missing out on everything the city has to offer? The energy? The vibrancy? I think you can love this place and love the city too—your cottage is a beautiful retreat, but don't make it a prison.'

His eyes were firmly fixed on the window, giving her space. She examined his features, wondering how it was he saw her so clearly, how he could make her see herself so clearly.

'Was it always difficult with your parents?' he asked eventually.

Maya sighed—he was going to keep picking away at this. And then she realised—this was what he'd been trying to do all along: help her to talk about the things that pained her the same way she'd helped him. He'd not always been subtle, and he'd not always been right, but he'd always been trying to help. And of course it all came down to this—to her past. Will had helped her see how her need to prove herself to her parents had infected every friendship, every relationship she had ever had.

She took a couple of slow, calming breaths before she answered his question. 'It was never really *difficult*. Not for them, at least.'

'What do you mean?'

'Well, they didn't want me around, so I never was. I had nannies. I was sent away to school. They bought me a house when I went to university so I wouldn't have to come home in the holidays.' She looked up and caught his fractionally raised eyebrow. 'I know how it sounds,' she said quietly. 'I know I had lots of material privileges. I was lucky I could use their money to start my business. But I would have traded it in if I could.'

'I know,' he said with a sympathetic smile and a squeeze to her hand. 'And what about your cooking?'

He really *did* understand her, she thought, touched that he knew exactly the right question to ask to get to the heart of the matter. The part of her story that had always hurt her most.

'I tried to talk to them about it once.'

Her voice was quiet as she remembered that night—how she'd prepared what she wanted to say, rehearsed it over and over in the car on the drive home. Arguments and counter-arguments and curveballs, all ready to fight her case.

'I wasn't enjoying university, and I was only getting by because I worked non-stop. I wanted to quit, to go to college and study culinary arts. I had this whole plan laid out, and I went to them and told them what I wanted to do. If they'd even told me that I wasn't to do it that would have been better, I think.'

'What *did* they say?'

'They said that I should do what I thought best. And would I be gone by seven because they were going out for dinner.'

He found her hand with his and squeezed. But Maya didn't feel the sadness and despair that this memory usually caused. Saying it aloud like that for the first time, she suddenly saw how outrageous her parents' behaviour had been. It occurred to her that their lack of interest was not because of anything she'd done, or hadn't done. They were just two very selfish people wrapped up in their own lives.

'And you stayed on the course?'

With a resigned sigh, she finished the story. 'I worked every minute for the next two years to get my first. They didn't even come to my graduation.'

'You know what?' he said. 'I wish I could say that deep down they're proud of what you've achieved here. But I don't know them, and I can't guess at how they feel. What I *do* know is that *you* should be proud of you. It's up to you what you're going to do with the rest of your life; whether you can leave their cruelty behind and start trying to please yourself.'

He was right. It wouldn't matter what she did, what she achieved. If she measured her success by what her parents thought of it she'd never be happy. She looked up at him, surprised and touched both by what he was saying and the fact he was saying it. She'd told herself that she wasn't going to think about what was happening between them until she was recovered from this migraine, but she couldn't help marvelling at this change and wondering what it would mean for them.

'It doesn't matter what they think,' he went on. 'It matters what *you* think.'

She stifled a yawn as she thought over his words, and looked out of the window at her little slice of English countryside. She thought of all the people she had taught and cooked for over the years. All the happiness she had brought people and how much happiness they'd inspired in her. She felt a warm glow of satisfaction and knew she couldn't be bitter, or angry, or sad about anything that had led her here.

'Actually, I think I'm doing okay. What about you?'

What about *him*? What did she mean? Did he think *she* was doing okay or *he* was doing okay? He pondered the question—the questions. If he'd known a month ago where he'd find himself sitting now he would have considered his present situation very *not* okay. He didn't get close to people. He didn't talk about his family. He didn't think about his family. It was a very small, but very firm set of principles that kept his life in check. And he had broken every one of them in the last week.

It had hurt. There had been times when he'd

known he hadn't experienced pain like it since Julia died. But when he tried to think of anything that had happened in the last year—the last ten years—that came close to how good kissing Maya had felt, he came up with nothing.

He opened his mouth to answer her, but she gave a little snuffle. She'd fallen asleep. And as he turned to look at her her head dropped and rested against his arm. He tried to extract his hand from hers without waking her, but then she rolled, trapping both their hands beneath her. He sat back, unsure what to do.

It wouldn't be right to stay like this, but it was so very tempting. For a start, after his sleepless night and draining day, the sight of any bed—even one without Maya in it—would tempt him almost beyond reason. With this bed, this woman, it would be nigh on impossible to walk away. She looked contented, though, and he smiled. He'd been worried that she would be upset, talking about her parents, but she seemed lighter, more relaxed. *Too* relaxed, he thought, watching her sleep and missing her company.

But getting into bed with an unconscious woman wasn't exactly his style. He pulled his hand out from under her slowly, trying not to disturb her. But her eyes drifted open and she seemed surprised to see him there.

'I was just going,' he said softly.

'Don't,' Maya whispered as her eyes drifted shut again, and threaded her fingers with his. 'Stay.'

Sagging back against the pillows, Will couldn't help but enjoy the feel of her body against his side. In five minutes...ten...when she was in a deeper sleep, he'd go.

But half an hour passed and he made no move to leave, too contented and peaceful to drag himself away. He'd thought he'd known peace before—before Maya. But now he could see that feeling for what it was: emptiness. He'd got through his days without feeling sad or angry, but the cost was never feeling joy or elation or love. This peace filled him, made his every cell feel alive. Eventually his eyes started to drift shut.

He woke briefly in the night, to find Maya curled tightly against him, an arm thrown across his belly; an ankle hooked around his, and he wrapped his arms around her waist, desperate to hold her close. As the sun slanted through the open window in the early hours Maya woke too.

He watched her as she drifted out of sleep, a small smile on her lips. Eventually she looked up.

She pulled back slightly and tilted her head, a sleepy, sensual smile teasing the corners of her mouth. He met her gaze head-on and his hand left her waist to drift slowly up her arm.

He wanted her. She looked beautiful. Crumpled and sleepy, but so candid. She wasn't playing games. Her joy at finding him there radiated from her face, and he was desperate to kiss her. But he couldn't do anything about it—not unless he knew it was really what she wanted. He knew what *he* wanted—her. All of her. All of the time. He had never imagined before that he could feel like that—that he could be overjoyed to realise it was what he wanted. He couldn't walk away from this. He couldn't sacrifice this joy because he was afraid.

'Are you awake?' he asked in a whisper, his breath disturbing the hair that had fallen across her face. He brushed it gently away.

'Yes,' she breathed, lifting her hand to his chest and closing her fingers around his shirt. Will's eyes dropped to her hand, and then moved back to her face. He thought he must be dreaming, that such a perfect moment couldn't possibly be real.

His hand drifted higher, brushing over her arm, her shoulder, until it rested on her jaw, where his thumb gently caressed her. As he brought her face towards him his gaze flickered from her lips up to her eyes, until Maya moaned softly, and he kissed her.

His lips moved slowly, tentative and gentle, and the kiss stayed sweet as they tested and explored. But even through the torrent of sensation assaulting his body he could feel Maya slipping away from him. Sleep was pulling at her, and he knew he had to let her go—for now. Only the thought that they would wake again in a few hours—here, together—and pick up where they left off soothed him.

'You're tired,' he said. A statement, not a question. 'Go back to sleep.' He kissed her gently on the forehead and tucked her head under his chin, and then locked both arms firmly around her waist.

Her bed was screaming.

Maya opened her eyes in a panic, trying to work

out where the noise was coming from. Darkness surrounded her and she realised that her face was pressed up against something warm and solid; she pushed at it with her hands but it fought back, pulling her down on the bed, refusing to let go. Suddenly claustrophobic, she struggled harder and sat up; it was only when she looked down that realisation struck. It was Will—in her bed. What the…?

'Morning,' she said hesitantly.

'Good morning,' Will replied, his face losing its sleepy, dreamy quality as he saw her. He look startled, awkward. 'Sorry, I forgot my alarm was set,' he said, jabbing at the screen of his phone until the noise stopped. 'You look much better today,' Will said, his voice a little brusque. 'How do you feel?'

'Honestly?' she replied, leaning back against the pillow. 'A little confused.'

His face fell, but as her gaze dropped to his lips she remembered—remembered every second of the kiss they had shared that morning…or last night…whenever it had been. But she couldn't think of what to say, and before she could find the right words her belly rumbled.

'You're hungry,' Will said shortly as he stood up.

She sat forward and rubbed the sleep from her eyes, trying to keep up. 'Just give me a minute to wake up properly and I'll make us some breakfast.'

'You will not.'

She tensed at his overbearing tone.

'It's fine,' she countered. 'You go ahead and I'll be down in a second.' She ran a hand through her hair and tried to sound calm, as if waking up with a man she was falling for was something that happened every day.

'Maya, *I'll* make a start on breakfast. No arguments. Come down when you're ready.'

He walked out of her bedroom before she had a chance to argue.

As soon as the door closed behind him Maya dropped her head into her hands. She couldn't be more mortified. She'd woken up wrapped around him like some crazy clingy woman, and now he had run at the first possible moment. It just didn't make sense. Her memories of that kiss were suffused with warmth, pleasure, delight. But she hadn't seen that Will in the man she'd woken up with this morning.

Well, no wonder, she told herself as she remembered the way she'd acted when she had first woken. She'd practically beaten her fists on his chest to get him to let her go. As if being sick in front of the man hadn't been bad enough.

She let out a groan, threw on some clean clothes and headed for the kitchen.

Will had found cereal and fruit and had laid the table for breakfast. A pot of tea sat on the countertop with a couple of mugs, and he'd even managed to find the milk jug. The boy learned fast. He emerged from the pantry and she gave him a cautious smile, uncertain whether to mention their kiss. Where would she start? She hadn't even had a chance to think about how *she* felt about it yet, never mind what she might want to say to *him* about it.

'This is nice,' she said lamely.

'It's nothing,' he replied. 'Sit. Eat.'

She did as she was told, trying to enjoy the novel experience of being fussed over, but Will's brusqueness was making her tense, nervous.

'So what are we doing today?' Will asked her, and a warm glow chased away her doubts.

He was staying. It was amazing, she thought, how the landscape of their relationship had changed so much that there wasn't even any question of him leaving before the week was up.

'I'm actually not sure,' Maya replied, relaxing slightly, hoping that a smile would improve his mood as well as hers. 'Yesterday threw me a bit. Let me check my notes for what we're meant to be cooking.'

'I didn't mean what are you going to teach me. I meant what are you going to do to recuperate?'

She looked up, and although his tone was sharp she saw concern, not anger in his features. She smiled wider: he was still trying to protect her.

'I'm done recuperating,' she said decisively, excited to embark on the day now that she knew that Will was staying. 'What I'm going to do is teach you to make coq au vin!' she said as her plans came back to her. 'And then I'm going to bake and ice a hundred fairy cakes.'

She could see him trying to decide whether to lecture her. But eventually his concerned expression cracked into a hint of a smile and she knew he was going to agree. *Good choice*, she thought. There was no way she could be kept out of the kitchen for two days in a row, and she loved that he understood that.

'Or you could teach *me* to bake and ice a fairy cake? By number ninety-nine I might have got the hang of it.'

'Do I have a choice in this?' she asked good-naturedly.

'Not really.'

He smiled, and it reached the pit of her stomach. She thought about everything he'd done for her yesterday—everything he'd seen and heard, the memories she must have stirred up. And he'd done it all for her. Agreeing with him now was the least she could do.

Will must have sensed her wavering: he spoke with a grin. 'I can pretend you do if it makes you feel better.'

CHAPTER NINE

WHY WAS HE offering to make fairy cakes? Why was he here, full-stop?

The answer was simple: Maya.

A few days ago his brain had been screaming at him to leave. But now, even knowing that there was a risk that one day he might get hurt, it wasn't. Not when the rewards of staying were so vast.

Being around Maya made him happy—happier than he'd ever felt before, he suspected. But that wasn't quite enough to quiet the voices. They were no longer screaming, and he was no longer going to obey unquestioningly, but that didn't mean that he could block them out completely.

And they had plenty to say this morning: about how scared he'd been yesterday when he'd thought Maya might be seriously ill. How painful it had been to sit in that bathroom with her and not be able to make her better.

The pain of losing Julia suddenly felt fresh in

his heart, and he was terrified of going through it again. Terrified that one day he might have to face the pain of losing Maya. And the closer she got, the worse it would be.

She'd lost him again. Maya eyed Will carefully, trying to squash her feelings of disappointment until she was sure. But there was no denying it: she hadn't noticed when it had happened, or what she'd said to cause it, but as she watched him methodically and purposefully cream butter and sugar she could tell he wasn't really there. She was determined not to panic; maybe he just needed space—time to adjust to everything that had happened last night, this morning.

He'd been withdrawing more and more all day, but even though he wasn't talking he was telling her more than he realised. She'd given him a list with the quantities of ingredients to weigh out, but after he'd done that he'd been the one to add the butter and sugar to the mixing bowl and pluck a wooden spoon from the jar of utensils.

She didn't say a word. Didn't even offer him the electric beaters for fear of disturbing whatever he was working through in his mind.

He'd looked up and met her eyes more than once, and she'd held her breath, wondering if this was the moment when he would come back to her, when he would open up and give them…whatever this was…a chance. But he'd always looked away, his jaw tense and his eyes regretful.

Everything that had tumbled into the open from the time his lips had met hers had been washed away from them, and she was frustrated and sad in equal measure. She couldn't begin to imagine the pain that Will must have felt at losing his family, but he wasn't the only one to have pain in his past. He couldn't just decide to disappear from the world because sometimes it was *hard*.

He had a choice here; if he really wanted to he could be happy. They could be happy together, she was sure. But not if he was going to keep running like this. He just needed the courage to try.

When he added a spoonful of flour with the first egg, to stop the mixture from splitting, the words escaped her before she could stop them.

'You've done this before.'

Will looked up suddenly, with a look on his face that told her he knew he'd been caught out.

'Neil had a sweet tooth,' he said, and then looked away.

She chanced a small smile. Her words had been a challenge and he'd not let her down. He could have ignored the question, he could have lied, but instead he'd told her the truth.

His eyes returned to the bowl and didn't leave it again as he gently folded in the flour. Maya resisted the urge to speak, not wanting to push her luck. After everything he'd told her about Julia, the pain that he'd faced, she couldn't imagine what more there was in his life that could hurt him. Neil had 'had' a sweet tooth, Will had said, and she wondered with a pang of sadness whether he'd lost his foster father too.

Later she watched as he iced perfect swirls on to the tops of the cakes. Neither of them had said a word for close to an hour. Maya had kept deliberately quiet: she knew him well enough now to judge when to push and when to give him space. She knew something else too: he'd come back to her. They'd been taking two steps forward and one step back since the minute that they'd met. Frustrating—yes, but going in the right direction.

She wished she could put her hand over his,

soothe him, but she knew he needed to do this, needed to think. A week ago she'd have been convinced she'd done something wrong, that she wasn't enough for him. Now she knew that wasn't true. It was his problems he was fighting, not her. But eventually she saw the fight leave his face, and she knew he was on his way back to her.

'I haven't seen him for fifteen years.'

She searched his face for clues, listened carefully to his tone, trying to work out what he wanted, whether he wanted her to ask more.

She chose her words thoughtfully, wanting to help and encourage, but not to pressure him.

'Was that what you wanted?'

'No.' His face was filled with raw emotion as he took a breath and then fixed her with his gaze. She knew why—knew how much stronger she felt when they were together, and that he must feel it too. 'He sent me back to the home. I didn't have a choice.'

Her arms ached with the need to pull him close, but she knew she couldn't do that. Will needed space, and to do this in his own time. He had just shown her that they weren't clear of the woods or their past yet.

He'd gone back to his icing, and the look on his face was so unlike anything she'd seen before. He was entirely focussed on making each one perfect. But not in the tense, white-knuckled way he had been when he'd first arrived.

She glanced around the kitchen, taking in the sight of boxed and iced fairy cakes covering almost every surface. There must be almost a hundred, she thought.

She was just about to ask Will if he wanted to call it a day when there was a knock at the front door.

'Gwen!' Maya exclaimed, surprised to find her neighbour on her doorstep—again.

'Maya, I'm *so* pleased you're home,' Gwen said, pushing past her through the doorway. 'I've got an emergency on my hands, again, I know—I'm sorry.'

She started to explain, but stopped when she saw Will emerge from the kitchen.

'Oh, you're still here,' she said, with a transparent smile at Maya. 'I heard you were both in the pub on Tuesday night.' She bumped Maya with her hip.

'You wanted to ask me something?' Maya

prompted, wanting to deflect her attention. Whatever was there between her and Will today it was too young, too fragile, to be scrutinised like that.

'Oh, yes. Well, I absolutely *have* to get to the office this afternoon and it will be a nightmare if I have to take the children. Could you watch them for me?'

Maya fixed a smile on her face, trying to think through her plans for the rest of the day. They *had* practically finished the cakes—there were only a handful left to ice—and she hadn't firmly decided on anything else for that evening.

'Um…'

She really didn't want to watch the children though. And she knew that this was her chance— her opportunity to make a stand. She had every reason to say no to Gwen. Her head might be just about back to normal, but her whole body felt exhausted. Definitely not up to the challenge of two under-fives. And she wanted space for her and Will too—space to see what might happen.

'They're just outside in the car,' Gwen went on. 'I told them to wait until I'd checked with you, but I'll go and get them now. Thanks, Maya. You're a life-saver.'

Maya squirmed. She knew she should say something. Will was right: this wasn't fair. But as her brain raced through what would happen if she said no she felt a gnawing anxiety in her gut. Would Gwen disappear from her life if she let her down? Would all her friends, if word spread? The spectre of that lonely existence hovered beside her as she shifted her feet, willing herself to speak.

Will cleared his throat and gave Maya a pointed look. Gwen turned back around at the sound, leaving Maya with no choice but to say something.

'Actually, Gwen...' she started, but didn't know how to continue. Will placed a warm, firm hand in the small of her back and pushed her forward half a step. She took a deep breath. 'Um...I don't think I can help today,' she said, her eyes fixed to the floor. 'I had a migraine, you see, and I'm still not quite recovered. I'm sorry.'

'Oh!' Gwen said, looking mildly embarrassed. 'I hadn't thought... Are you okay?'

Maya nodded quickly, knowing a blush was rising on her cheeks. 'Better than yesterday.'

'Well, don't worry about it at all,' Gwen said. 'You look after yourself. And call me if you need anything.'

'Wait,' Maya called as Gwen reached the door. 'We've almost finished the cakes, if you want to take them with you now?'

'You've finished them already?' Gwen asked. 'Maya, you're an angel.'

'See—not so hard,' Will said as Gwen drove away and they both stepped back to close the door.

Maya turned sharply to face him, her hands planted on her hips, furious.

'You didn't have to do that, you know. I'm perfectly capable of making up my own mind.' She'd been giving him space all afternoon, not pushing more than she thought he could take, and then he just blundered in and practically forced her to tell Gwen no when she'd not even had a chance to think it through.

'Did you *want* to look after her children?' Will's voice was infuriatingly reasonable as he leant back against the door and watched her.

'I wouldn't have minded,' she lied.

'Really? After yesterday, did you really want to watch someone else's children? Again?'

That was hardly the point, Maya thought, though she wasn't sure who she was trying to convince.

It was exactly the point. It was everything Will
had been trying to show her since she'd arrived.
Everything she'd come to see was true about the
way she was living her life. But she would have
got there on her own; she'd have told Gwen no
eventually. Probably.

'Maya, I'm not sure why you're angry,' Will
said, his voice irritatingly calm.

Anger prickled under her skin and she knew it
should be aimed at herself. That she'd fallen at this
first opportunity to stand up for herself. But Will
stood there looking so smug, as if it was the easi-
est thing in the world to change, when he'd been
fighting against it since the moment they'd met.

'I only wanted to remind you what we'd talked
about,' he said. 'You were going to say yes when
you wanted to say no.'

How did he see through her like that? Through
everything she did to the decade-old heartache beneath? How could he hit so quickly on her fears,
make her so vulnerable? Her heart pounded and
she could feel the adrenaline coursing through her
veins as she threw her anger at him, desperately
trying to direct it away from herself.

'And what gives you the right to interfere?' she

demanded. 'What gives you the right to tell me anything about how to live my life?'

'You know exactly why.'

He raised his voice to compete with hers, his shoulders tensing now. He was surprised, she guessed, at the turn the conversation had taken.

'Because... Because I—' He stopped abruptly.

Maya waited for a beat—waited for him to finish that sentence. When he didn't, she couldn't resist. 'Because you *what*?'

Suddenly Will's expression softened and he smiled at her, shrugging.

'Because I care, okay? Because when I see someone hurting you reason flies out of the window and I can't stop myself from caring. Is that what you want to hear?'

Maya stared at him, shocked into silence; her anger dissipated in an instant.

'Are you going to say anything?' Will asked.

'Thank you for being honest,' Maya said carefully, knowing it wasn't really enough—not after the way he'd laid himself bare.

She couldn't even begin to think what to say back. That she cared about him too? Well, of course she did; he must know that. But one thought above all others won her attention, and she knew she couldn't ignore what had happened any longer. She had been so certain it was real when those memories had flooded back. But maybe they hadn't—maybe it was fantasy. Either way, she had to know.

'Will, about last night…'

He looked at her intently, but didn't rush to fill any blanks.

'I woke up and you were there…and…' She took a deep breath, thought back to those magical few minutes in the small hours of that morning—how right it had felt to be in his arms, how perfectly they'd understood each other. It *was* real—it had to be. 'I know I didn't imagine it.'

A smile crept up from the corners of Will's mouth as he took a step towards her. 'You didn't imagine it,' he said, and the smile finally reached his eyes. 'It was real. Very real.'

He leaned in close and brushed his lips against hers. Even this, the briefest of caresses, set off sparks that lit her up from the soles of her feet to her hair.

'I was worried you didn't remember. That you weren't really awake,' he said.

'It took me a minute to wake up. Mornings aren't my best time.'

'I'll have to remember that,' Will murmured.

The suggestive glint in his eye made her blush, but his implication that there would be more mornings to come—the first hint that this could be something real, something lasting—glowed in her heart.

'So what shall we do this evening?' she asked, still finding it wondrous that he was really here, *present*, with her.

'I'm going to make you dinner while you take it easy.'

The easy confidence of his voice told Maya she'd no choice in the matter. But instead of instantly dismissing the idea of being waited on she sat with the thought for a moment, tried to imagine what that would feel like.

'Am I just meant to watch you slave over a hot stove? I'm not allowed to help at all?'

'You're not allowed to do anything,' he told her. 'When was the last time anyone made you dinner?'

She knew the look on her face told him everything he needed to know.

'Precisely,' he said, a little smug. 'No arguments.'

'Okaaay…' she replied hesitantly.

She'd let him have his way. She'd give his idea a try as he had trusted her so often this week. It was impossible to deny this happy, easy-going Will just about anything. It delighted her to see him like this, so close to carefree.

But she knew being in the kitchen was hard for him, and they'd already spent hours there. 'It's still early. How about a walk first?'

They wandered through the garden and out across the meadow, heading for the river. Will stayed close by her side, and the occasional brush of his arm against hers, the touch of his hand under her elbow, created layer upon layer of awareness in her body.

Her skin tingled with anticipation, almost as if there was some sort of charge between them— some energy that was only satisfied when they were touching, when it could explode. Their gazes met occasionally, and the looks that passed between them seemed to travel from his eyes directly to her chest, constricting her lungs, making her gasp for air, until he looked away and she could breathe again.

Eventually they reached the path between a leafy avenue of trees and Maya paused, as she always did there, to look back at her cottage. The bright afternoon sun played on the walls, soaking life into the old stones, and the sea of colour in the meadow shifted and changed with every breath of the light summer wind. She let out a deep sigh of contentment and closed her eyes, tipping her face up to the warmth of the sun. She thought, as she did every day, how lucky she was to have found a place that had brought her such happiness and peace. But Will was right. Just because she was happy here it didn't mean it was the *only* place she could be happy.

He moved behind her, and when he settled his hands on her shoulders she relaxed into them, revelling in the knowledge that she could do this. That he was offering her all he had to give, was hers for the taking. His hands slid round her waist and pulled her back tightly; he pressed a kiss to the side of her neck.

'It really is beautiful here,' he murmured.

Maya shifted slightly in his arms, so her forehead rested gently against his jaw. Will's lips pressed to her temple and she couldn't stop a quiet moan from escaping her. His hands caressed her waist, smoothing the curves of her sides, sweeping low over her belly, while his lips continued to tease at her hairline. Biting her lip, almost breathless with expectation, she closed her eyes, succumbing to the surfeit of sensation. Will's hands settled on her hips, heavier than before, and he turned her firmly before sneaking his arms back around her and holding her tight.

His caressing lips found her mouth at last. But the touch of his lips on hers brought her up short. Happy as she was, she wasn't delusional. She knew there were still things they had to face, still hurts to overcome, before Will would be ready to commit to this—whatever *this* was. This morning they had shared a kiss just as sweet as this, and it had not stopped him from disappearing into himself a few hours later.

She pushed her hands against his chest and took a step away from him. Her breathing was heavy, and her arms itched to loop themselves around Will's neck. But she knew that she couldn't let herself. If Will wanted her he had to stop holding back. She hadn't wanted to confront Gwen—not today, not yet. But with help from him she'd done it. And now it was over she felt lighter, freer, and knew that it had been the right thing. She needed the same from Will. She knew there were parts of his story he was still holding back, and if he wasn't prepared to step up, as she had, then they were better off walking away from each other now.

'Maya?' said Will, rubbing at the back of his neck, no doubt confused by her sudden change of mood.

'I'm sorry,' she said as she turned and walked on, down towards the river.

'What is it?' he asked, catching up with her. 'What's wrong?'

She psyched herself up to ask the question she knew they had to face. If they were going to pursue this attraction, this bond that was so tangible between them, she had to know that Will was being open with her, that he wasn't still holding back.

'You mentioned your foster father earlier. I'd like to know about him.'

'Now?' he asked, following closely behind her. His voice was unsteady and he reached for her shoulder. 'That's what you were thinking just now? That you want to know about my *parents*?'

'I want to know *you*.' She reached up and brushed her fingertips across his cheek, meeting his eyes and smiling softly. All the time she wondered if he would see the real question behind her words: *Are you really ready for this?*

CHAPTER TEN

HE HADN'T MEANT to shut her out this afternoon. Hadn't meant to retreat to that quiet, still, cold place in his mind. But he'd been shocked by her reaction when she woke. She hadn't seemed to want him close, so he'd given her space. And then, when he'd started with the cakes, the world had just sort of faded. His hands had got on with the job with little input from him: they'd seemed to remember well enough from long hours in the kitchen with Julia.

But then Gwen had shown up at the door and he'd known he had to help Maya to stand up for herself. He couldn't bear to see her beaten down by her own dizzying expectations of herself. She had been so close he'd only needed to lend her a little support. But that hadn't been enough. It would never be enough. Because once he'd done it he'd had to think about why. And the reason was so clear that he couldn't avoid it.

He cared about her.

And now he had to give more. *Again.* She wanted to know about Neil. The last piece of himself he'd been able to keep from confronting, locked away, secure, where it couldn't hurt him. And he knew that he was out of chances. To push her away after what they had shared last night would be cruel. This was final. If he wanted any sort of future with Maya he had to step up.

He didn't know what he wanted from *her.* Didn't know how much he could risk. But he knew that if she decided today that she wanted nothing more to do with him he would despair. If talking would stop that happening—give him more space, more time to try and work out what it was that was happening—he would do it.

He dropped down onto a fallen tree trunk by the side of the river and started to speak, his arms resting on his knees.

'After Julia died Neil and I tried to carry on.'

He tried his usual trick, distancing himself from the words as if he was telling someone else's story. But as he spoke he could see the scenes in his mind. See his fifteen-year-old self, lonely and afraid, and his heart broke. He felt the full force of his words now. There was no hiding, no pretending. His words hurt, but he could see past them, see past the pain to what was waiting on the other side: Maya.

'But when I looked at Neil it was as if he wasn't there. I never understood at the time what he was going through. I'd never loved anyone like he loved Julia. I thought that he didn't care.'

Maya leaned against him and he took comfort from her. He knew that however bad his memories were, they were in the past. Maya was *here. Now.*

'Oh, Will, I'm sure he loved you,' she said gently. 'It sounds as if he wasn't well.'

'I'm starting to see that.' Yesterday, when Maya had been ill, he'd had the tiniest insight into what Neil might have been feeling, and for the first time he'd started to appreciate the magnitude of his foster father's grief.

He'd been thinking about Neil more and more. It would be so simple and yet so hard to see him again, to speak to him. But part of Will wanted to—to see if he could recapture a part of those happy years of his childhood. But what if Neil didn't want him? What if he was rejected, again?

Will dropped his head into his hands and rubbed

at his hair. When he lifted his head one hand stayed at his neck, trying to rub away the tension. He watched the water ripple and the light play on its surface, filtering through the trees.

'So what happened after that?' Maya asked eventually.

A week ago he would have bristled, been angry at anyone prying into his personal life. But he knew that Maya wasn't being nosy, wasn't trying to push. She just wanted to know him.

'Oh, we carried on for a little while,' he explained, his heart heavy as he remembered those horrendous weeks. 'But one day my social worker turned up, asked me a lot of questions and spent a long time locked away with Neil. And then I was off back to the group home.' He tried to sound flippant, but the memory of that day hit him hard in the gut, a physical pain, and his voice broke.

'I'm so sorry.'

Her voice was soft, caring. And it gave him the strength he needed to carry on.

'Losing Julia taught me how much it hurt to lose someone you love.'

He tried to control his voice. Breathed deeply, looking for the calm he'd spent years working on, the new peace he'd found with Maya. It was no-where to be found, so he just forced the words out as best he could.

'She was pulled from me, and I took some comfort in knowing that she didn't want to go any more than I wanted her to leave. But Neil? At the time it felt like he just didn't care. Didn't love me enough. I knew I couldn't give anyone that power over me again.'

'And that's why—'

'And that's why meeting you terrified me,' he said with a small smile. 'I've never met anyone in my life so impossible to resist.'

'I didn't do it on purpose.'

Her voice was small, worried, and he squeezed her hand, pressed it to his cheek.

'I know, I know.'

He looked up and the sight of her, her red hair and purple dress and bright green eyes, instantly lightened him. When he leaned across and brushed his lips gently across hers more weight fell, and his arm drifted up and around her shoulders.

'I chased you here,' he said, the corners of his mouth turning up. He was amazed that he could smile with his memories so close by. 'I think we have established that beyond any doubt.'

She smiled back at him and then rested her head against his shoulder, looking out over the water.

He had no secrets from Maya now—was completely vulnerable to her. Without doubt, if she wanted to, she could break his heart as soundly as Neil had done. But that knowledge didn't sit heavily on his shoulders. He only felt excited, exhilarated that she could have that effect on him. He should be terrified, but when he saw the light catch the gold in her hair, saw the corners of her mouth turn up at some silent thought, he couldn't regret it.

'There's actually something I need to tell *you*,' Maya said eventually, her words lazy and relaxed.

'Oh?' He sounded worried.

'It's nothing bad. It's just…' She took a deep breath, knowing that she was giving him permission to leave. 'You know that I'll cater your dinner, don't you? It doesn't matter if you don't want to finish the course.'

Her heart fell at the look of unbridled relief and happiness that crossed his face.

'Maya, thank you.' His voice was full of delight, and she cringed at the sound of it. 'You have no idea what that means to me. *Thank you.*'

She bit her lip. She hadn't been prepared for him to be quite so thrilled about the prospect of leaving. Of course she'd thought briefly that maybe he wouldn't stay now that he didn't have to, but his being so pleased by the idea was devastating.

Will must have caught the look on her face, because he trapped it between his palms.

'What's wrong?'

'Nothing,' she lied, trying to hide her heartbreak. 'It's nothing. I guess you were only here because of Sir Cuthbert anyway.'

It had hurt, knowing that was the only reason he had come, but she had thought that what had developed between them was real. That how they'd got here together in the first place wasn't so important. She tried to turn away, cast a glance up at the cottage. She wished they were back up there, so she could escape somewhere, have some privacy.

'You think I'm *going*?'

The incredulous look on Will's face eased the fist gripping her heart.

'Aren't you?'

'No.' He said the word slowly, deliberately. 'I'm staying. I promise.'

She looked up and met the intensity of his gaze head-on. Once her eyes had locked on his she couldn't look away, not until his lips met hers, and she let them drift shut as she drowned in sensation.

He was staying. She still couldn't quite make herself believe it as they started back towards the house. Her heart wanted to soar, but she kept a firm grip on it. He had made no promises for the future, no avowals of love. All she knew—all he had promised her—was the rest of this week.

She shook her head, clearing her thoughts, determined to concentrate on what she did have right now.

'So what culinary delights do I have in store for me tonight?' she asked.

'Ah…'

Maya guessed that Will hadn't thought quite that far ahead in his plan.

'Well, I hadn't thought about the details yet, but I'm sure I can—'

'It doesn't matter. I can cook. Or we can do it together.'

'No. I'm meant to be giving you a break, remember? I'm cooking, and you're going to let me.'

She fought against the urge to argue, to insist, determined to trust him, to give herself a chance to live differently.

'Okay. You know where the fridge is, and there are recipe books on the dresser if you want inspiration.'

He nodded thoughtfully. 'I should keep it simple,' he said. 'I made a cottage pie once. For Julia's birthday—my first time solo in the kitchen. Think I can manage it again?'

Maya smiled, touched that he was making a meal that meant so much to him and by the way he had just dropped Julia's name into conversation. 'I trust you.'

Three hours, seven saucepans, two courses and a visit to the first aid box later, Maya let out a deep, contented breath, leaning back in her seat.

'I'm impressed, Will. Seriously.' She laid down her spoon and fork. Her bowl was scraped clean.

'I know. You've already said that. Twice.' He tried to keep the smugness from his face, but he looked unbelievably thrilled that he had managed to do this for her. For him too.

'But I think back to that first night and—'

He groaned. 'I know I was a pain that night.'

'Not on purpose.'

'No, but I didn't really try to *not* be a pain either.'

'Let's forget about it.' Maya smiled and stood to clear the bowls, but found herself trapped by a strong arm around her waist. 'Will, I'm just clearing these—'

Words deserted her as he twisted his chair and pulled her towards him so she was trapped between his thighs.

'I know this has been difficult,' he said earnestly. 'That *I* have been difficult.'

'You stayed,' she said simply, trying to think straight through the onslaught on sensation she felt at being in his arms. 'That tells me all I need to know. The fact that you're still here, however difficult it is.'

His legs closed more firmly around hers and his hand found the nape of her neck as he pulled her into his lap. Her eyes closed as she leaned towards him, her tongue moistening her bottom lip. She held her breath, suddenly nervous, unsure, wondering whether this man could truly give her what she needed, whether he was ready for a relationship.

His lips touched against hers, slow, sweet and gentle. She kissed him back instinctively, and heat spread from every point that their bodies met.

After everything Will had told her today she shouldn't be having doubts. He'd trusted her with secrets she was sure he'd never shared with anyone. But she wasn't his therapist. She was his lover. Or she could be. But even with everything they'd talked about there was one subject where she was still in the dark. How did he feel about her? Okay, he'd told her that she was difficult to resist. But he *had* spent the week resisting. Who was to say he wouldn't change his mind?

She deserved nothing less than love and commitment and honesty from the people in her life. No holding back, no playing games. He had shown her that.

Will pulled back and opened his eyes, sensing her hesitation.

'Maya, what is it?' he asked, cupping her face with one hand, brushing her hair back with the other.

She quivered, her every nerve-ending straining

for his caress. 'It's nothing,' she said quickly. But then paused, reconsidered. 'No, it's everything. I don't know, Will. I'm just not sure that this is a good idea.'

'Why?' His arms dropped to tighten around her waist.

It was hard to think when he was so close, and her body was urging her on. But she couldn't let herself be persuaded into this if it wasn't right.

'Because I'm not sure how you feel about me,' she said firmly. 'I'm not pushing you to tell me. I'm just not sure that I can do this without knowing.'

He looked floored, and she knew that he hadn't expected her question.

He opened his mouth to speak a couple of times before he finally forced some words out. 'I don't know what I can say to explain.'

She could hear his frustration in every word— not with her, but with himself. 'I've never... I just don't know... You're just so...'

He fell silent, exasperated, and she could see him sorting through words in his head.

He tried again. 'I think that...I'm trying to...I just...*love* you.'

She let out a gasp and sat up straight—and watched as the realisation of what he'd said hit him. His eyes widened and his mouth opened, but he didn't rush to deny the words. Instead as the shock faded it was replaced with a dazed smile.

'I...' She knew she should say something, but she'd no idea what.

Of course she was falling in love with him. But after the shock of his admission just saying his words back to him didn't seem right. It wasn't even the fact that he loved her that had shocked her so much. It was the fact that he had told her. She knew he'd never said those words to anyone. Understood how much of a risk he was taking by saying them to her.

'Will...' She tried starting again, then realised she didn't have to say anything; she could *show* him how she felt. Show him how much his words meant to her.

Leaning forward, she pressed her lips against his.

As soon as she did so Will's arms tightened around her again.

'I've been wanting to do this all evening,' he confessed breathlessly between kisses.

Maya moaned softly as he shifted her on his lap, his hands moving down from her waist to her hips, gripping her tightly. Her heartbeat thudded in her ears and she gasped, breathless.

'Me too,' she admitted. 'But I didn't think...'

'I know. I'm an idiot,' he said.

She wanted to laugh. Wanted to rejoice that this man, who just a few days ago had seemed so determined to hide himself from her, was here, with his arms around her, laughing, loving her. His fingers skirted the neckline of her sundress and came to rest on the top button; she arched into him, more sure than she'd ever been that she wanted to make love with him. Perhaps this would be one area where he could teach her a thing or two about the sensual.

His lips left the trail they were making up the side of her neck and he whispered urgently in her ear. 'Upstairs?'

She held her breath as she nodded, and then let out a squeal of surprise as Will stood from the chair, taking her with him.

'You're sure?' he asked, pausing as they reached the top step.

'Of course,' she whispered. 'I've barely thought of anything else this week. You've no idea—'

'Oh, you'd be surprised,' Will replied, kicking the door closed behind them.

Maya stirred beneath the blankets and stretched to ease the delicious ache that had invaded every muscle. As a cool breeze brushed across her cheek she realised something was wrong. She reached across the bed at the same time as she opened her eyes. The other side of the bed was still warm, but unmistakably empty.

She lifted herself up onto her elbows and fear curled instinctively in her belly. Only the dent in the pillow suggested anyone else had been there at all. For a moment she was unsure if she'd imagined the whole thing. But the trail of her clothes from the door to the bed convinced her otherwise. Will had been here—that much was certain. The question was, where was he now?

She felt empty as she acknowledged the question, because gut instinct had told her the answer. She lay still, trying to listen for the whistle of the kettle or the creak of a stair. Eventually she heard footsteps downstairs. Not the quiet padding of bare feet but the purposeful thump of shoes. She knew she had to get up, out of bed, but she hesitated. Once she did that—went down there and faced him—she wouldn't be able to kid herself any longer.

When Will didn't miraculously reappear, she climbed out of bed. And when she reached the bottom of the stairs and saw the suitcase propped by the front door she knew what a mistake she'd made. Her knees weakened and her shoulders slumped as the truth of the situation hit her and nausea rose from her gut. He'd promised her he wasn't leaving, and—stupidly—she'd believed he had a reason to stay.

It was Will who had shown her how she let people use her, take advantage of her to get what they needed. After everything he'd said she hadn't thought Will capable of doing the same thing. But the evidence made it clear how wrong she was.

Will emerged from the kitchen and jumped at the sight of her standing on the bottom step.

'Maya...'

He spoke slowly, warily, and Maya knew her face must be broadcasting her hurt and her anger. When had she ever been able to keep anything like that hidden from Will? His betrayal was absolute—could not have been designed to hurt her more. Her thoughts spun as she stumbled on the stair and leaned against the banister for support.

'I'm sorry,' he said, and she recognised the tone, the blankness in his eyes.

Some time between falling asleep in his arms and waking alone she'd lost him. No, she hadn't lost him—he'd left her. He was walking away, as if this week, last night, had meant nothing. She struggled to swallow, to breathe, to see.

'But you're going?' She forced the words out. The case by the door told her everything that she needed to know.

'I have to.'

She opened her mouth to protest, but couldn't find words as she realised that he was going to break her. It was so much worse than she had imagined it would be. She had let him into her heart and now he would tear his way out. It burnt like acid, radiating from her chest to every atom of her body. She couldn't have spoken even if she'd been able to think; she choked on her grief.

Eventually she managed one word. 'Explain.'

'I don't have time to explain, Maya.' His shoulders were tight, tense, and his eyes moved constantly between her, the door, the clock on the wall. 'The hospital just called. Neil's been rushed in with—chest pains. I have to go. Now.'

The lump cleared from her throat and breath was expelled from her chest in a rush. She sucked in oxygen, relief and sympathy flooding her body. This was not what she'd feared. He was frightened. He was in a hurry. He needed her support—not her anger.

'Oh, Will, I'm so sorry,' she said, turning suddenly and heading up the stairs, her hands trying to comb out her hair as she went. 'Let me just throw something on and I'll come with you.'

'No.'

'I'll be less than a minute, I swear. We'll be out through the door in less than three.' She looked down at the robe she'd thrown on upstairs. 'I just need to grab some jeans or—'

'I said *no*, Maya.'

She stumbled and sat heavily on the stairs as his words stopped her heart and her breath. The cruelty of his words, his actions, tore at her insides and she choked back tears.

'I'm going now,' he continued. 'And I don't want you to come.'

She tried to keep hopeful, to remind herself of what he was going through—the news he had just received—and tried to tell herself that she could understand. He was hurting and lashing out, that was all. He needed her to help him through this.

She gathered herself up, forced herself to a shaky stand, and walked back down the stairs. She reached him and laid a hand gently on his arm.

'I know you're scared.' She forced calm into her voice, tried to hide her fear and hurt. 'But it will be okay. You'll be okay, whatever happens. We'll deal with it together.'

'No!'

He practically spat the word this time, and she recoiled as if he had burnt her.

'Will, I love you. I want to help you. Tell me what I can do?'

He was already at the door, and as he reached for the handle he looked back over his shoulder at her.

'I'm sorry, Maya,' he said, and she knew from the flatness of his voice that he'd already left her. 'But this was a mistake.'

As the door slammed behind him she leaned

back against the newel post, letting it take her weight as she slid down to the floor. Grief blurred her vision and she wrapped her arms tight around her body, trying to hold herself together.

Sitting at the bottom of the stairs, Maya tried to understand what had happened, what had led them here. From the minute Will Thomas had walked into that office she'd known exactly where this would lead if she let her guard down. She wanted to scream at the woman she'd been a week ago. Rail at her; tell her never to let him into her heart or her home. Because this was how it had always been going to end: with her heart torn, broken, and him walking away without a backward glance.

Will had told her he loved her—he had promised her he would stay. The scale of his betrayal made it hard to breathe. In the end she had meant nothing to him. She had offered him everything, given him everything, and when she'd told him she loved him he'd brushed the words off as if they were nothing—as if *she* were nothing.

But she'd learnt her lesson now. He could be sure of that. This was it—the last time she would allow anyone to push her around, treat her like a doormat, take advantage. For days Will had been telling her to stand up for herself. She forced the racing of her heart into anger, channelled her desperation into determination. She would never allow this to happen again. It ended now.

CHAPTER ELEVEN

WILL RAISED HIS arms above his head and stretched, wishing it was as easy to soothe the ache in his heart. In the bed, riddled with wires and tubes, Neil slept soundly—as he had since Will had arrived that morning. Watching him, Will felt a mixture of relief and hope; above all, he was grateful that Neil was going to be okay.

A sensation of *déjà vu* had stalked Will since the moment he'd arrived at the hospital. The stale air, the whiff of antiseptic, the scuffed paint along the walls—it felt as if nothing had changed in the fifteen years since Julia had died here. As he'd walked through the corridors he'd clenched his fists, fighting off the surge of adrenaline that had kicked his heart into racing and made his limbs twitchy. He'd had to focus—get to Neil before it was too late.

When he'd heard that Neil was going to be fine the panic and the fear had receded like mist from a warm morning. As adrenaline had drained and his mind had cleared Will had truly understood for the first time what he'd done. He'd lost Maya. No. That would imply some accident, some unfortunate event. He hadn't lost her. He'd pushed her from him.

Bile rose in his throat as he remembered. He'd been cruel and callous. Vicious. He hadn't meant to be. Hadn't planned it. But the end result was the same. She was never going to talk to him again. Guilt churned his stomach as the scene replayed over and over in his mind, and grief tore at his heart at the thought that he might never see her again.

All he had been able to think about in those few minutes before he'd left the house was getting to the hospital as quickly as he could. Holding everything together until he got to Neil. All he had felt was fear. When he'd thought he might lose Neil again he'd remembered all too clearly why he'd made himself those rules that he had. *This* was the reason he didn't let anyone close. *This* was the pain that ruled his nightmares. He'd looked down at Maya and been overwhelmed by the strength of his love—and he'd remembered why he was so scared of this. The enormous price one paid for loving another person. He'd been terrified.

And yet… He was in pain now anyway.

Because the thought of never seeing Maya again—and why would she ever allow him close now?—filled him with despair. All he could see of his future without her was a dark, empty space.

The ironic thing was, if the call had come before he'd met Maya he probably wouldn't even have listened to the nurse, never mind come running. But he'd picked up the phone and when the nurse had mentioned Neil's name he'd risen and snatched up his clothes without thinking. As soon as he'd heard the words 'chest pains' he'd thought 'heart attack', and had known that he would never forgive himself if he didn't try to see Neil again. Make sense of what had happened between them. Make peace with it as well.

He'd been ready to leave in less than fifteen minutes.

The emotions that had coursed through him had been terrifying. And then there was Maya, telling him she loved him. Reminding him that now there was another person to fear losing. In that moment he had panicked. He'd felt his heart racing, his blood pumping, and above it all the cold, metallic taste of fear. And he'd thought that this was better. Better than letting her into his life and having her ripped from him later.

By the time he'd arrived Neil was out of danger and sleeping. The doctor had explained that he had had a severe angina attack but that it was under control now. Will knew that he couldn't leave until he'd spoken to Neil. It had taken a near tragedy to get him to realise it, but this was his family—the only family he had—and he couldn't walk away. And all this was because of Maya—because he'd learnt to love again, learnt how to share his life with another person.

He stood and walked over to the window: he needed something to watch, to occupy his mind. He thought of Maya at her cottage. The way she could sit and look out across the countryside, letting the calm and quiet wash over her. He'd thought that he'd found peace, too, with her. And then in one moment of fear and panic he'd destroyed any chance that he might have had. Because the last ten anguished hours had taught him one thing: he couldn't see a way to be happy again without her. Any thought of a future without Maya in it...he just couldn't face it.

He whipped his head round at the rustle of a sheet and the beeping of an alarm and his heart raced with panic. Neil was struggling in the bed, clawing at one of his tubes. Will hurried to his side without thinking, acting on instinct, out of love. He hit the call button for the nurse and then looked down and met Neil's eyes. His struggling stopped instantly and Will reached for his hand, moving it away from the tubes.

'It's fine,' Will told him, trying to keep his voice steady, even braving a smile. 'You're in hospital, but you're going to be fine.' He breathed out an enormous sigh as he said the words and for the first time truly believed them.

Neil's gaze flickered over Will and realisation, hope, and finally something he could only describe as joy crossed his foster father's face. Neil's smile broadened as he realised that Will was truly there.

'You're here,' Neil said weakly, his eyes still wide.

The nurse arrived then, and pushed Will back from the bed. He fiddled with his phone as he waited, suddenly feeling reticent, a little embar-

rassed about the way he'd walked in and just expected everything to be the same as it once was.

By the time the nurse left Neil was sitting up,
looking if not entirely healthy then a darn sight
better than he had half an hour ago. Will recognised the familiar humour in his eyes and the way
his mouth naturally settled into a smile. He had
not seen him like this since long before Julia had
died, Will realised with a shock. It was another
reminder of how ill Neil had been back then.

He had worried that conversation would be
awkward—how could it not be after all that had
passed? But no sooner had Neil started to apologise for everything that had happened than Will
stopped him. What Neil had gone through was no
more his fault that Julia's cancer had been hers.
Will knew that now. And having come so close to
losing Neil completely, before they'd been able to
make amends, he knew it was the future that was
important now—not raking over the past.

Later, Will found himself with his phone in his
hand, his eyes automatically checking for a 'new
message' symbol, knowing even as he did so that
hope was futile. He didn't even remember taking

it out of his pocket, but he was so desperate to hear from Maya he couldn't help himself.

'I've told you, Will. I'm fine now. If you need to be at work I know you're very busy…'

'No, it's not work,' he replied soberly, unable to keep the anguish from his voice.

'Ah, I see. Who is she, then?'

Will shifted uncomfortably in his chair. He'd forgotten how Neil could do that—see through whatever front he constructed. Sense every secret he was trying to hide. He rubbed his forehead with the heel of his hand, wondering if he could tell Neil everything that had happened, whether he would judge him for the terrible way he'd treated Maya this morning.

'Come on, Will. Let's have it.'

Suddenly Will felt fifteen again, being quizzed about why he was home an hour after curfew, smelling of perfume.

'You couldn't hide anything from me when you were a teenager, son; I don't know what makes you think you can get away with it now.'

Son. It had been a long time since he'd been called that. A very long time. But even with a hiatus of fifteen years it sounded right, somehow. Through the fog of black, he felt a warm glow of hope.

He had his family back. But it had cost him Maya, and broken her heart too.

He gave a long sigh. 'I've done something terrible.'

Will sat beside Neil's bedside and checked his watch. Eight o'clock. His phone had stayed resolutely still and silent all afternoon and into the evening, but he checked the screen again—just in case.

He didn't even raise his hopes; it was more habit than expectation. But now he knew that Neil was going to be okay all he could think about was how he could start to put things right with Maya. He called her again, even though he didn't expect her to answer. After all, she'd not picked up any of his calls all day. Worry ate at him, and his hands and thoughts were in constant motion.

He had to see her—had to try and make things right. He might have lost Neil today, and he couldn't bear the thought that he might lose her too. He had to apologise—make her see how disgusted he was with himself for the things that he had said.

Will said goodbye to Neil, who pulled him into a hug when he tried to shake his hand, and promised to visit soon. Then he walked down to the car park, fighting himself with every step not to break into a run.

When he reached the end of Maya's lane he stopped and tried to gather his chaotic thoughts, tried to calm the frenzy of emotion in his breast. What would he say if, by some miracle, Maya answered the door and let him speak? He knew that sorry wasn't enough. One word couldn't possibly fix the damage he had done.

All the way up the motorway he'd been trying to think of the magic words that would make her see what she meant to him, make her understand everything that he loved about her, realise how disgusted he was by the way he had behaved. But he hadn't found them. Hadn't been able to think of anything that would make good the fact that he'd promised to stay and been gone before breakfast.

The sound of her feet padding through the hallway heightened his nerves. His palms pricked with sweat and his heart pounded as he waited for her to open the door. The long pause between the silence of her footsteps and the turn of the key told him one thing: she knew he was here and she was preparing for confrontation. He could almost hear the deep breath she must be taking as she lifted the latch. He took one of his own.

She swung the door wide, but stood unmoving in the doorway and didn't say a word. There was pain written across her face, and a puffiness around her eyes that told him she'd been crying. He felt a twist of pain in his guts, knowing that he had done that. He'd do anything, he knew, to make this—her—okay again. He wanted her to be happy more than anything else. Even more than he wanted her back.

Eventually he swallowed down the lump in his throat.

'What do you want?' She held her head high and spoke slowly, evenly.

She sounded strong, he thought, so different from the raging of torrid emotion he was battling through to get his words out. 'Maya, I'm so sorry about earlier.'

'I didn't answer my phone,' she said, with a grit he hadn't seen in her before, 'because I didn't want to speak to you. Not because I wanted you to turn up here. I thought that would be obvious.'

She paused, and he could see indecision in her eyes.

'How's Neil?' she added, and he thanked heaven that she even cared enough to ask, in awe again at the extent of her incredible compassion.

'He's going to be okay. It was angina, not a heart attack. He's going to be fine. I had to see you. I had to explain.'

Her steely calm highlighted the warring of emotions in his chest, the sensation of losing his grip on his life, on everything he'd thought he knew and understood.

'You had plenty of time to explain this morning, Will.' She crossed her arms a little tighter—protecting herself, he saw, pushing him further away. 'Now? Now I'm not interested. I think it would be best if you left.'

'I love you, Maya. I can't take back this morning, but if you let me tr—'

'No.'

Will stopped dead at the power and certainty in her voice. He felt sick. Of course she was right. He wished he could go back, start the day over.

He hadn't left because he didn't love her, but he didn't know how he could ever make her believe that. It had been such a long time since he'd had anyone in his life that he'd forgotten how much his actions affected others. How he had the power to hurt people as much as they could hurt him.

'No,' she said again. 'I deserve better than how you treated me this morning. You're the one who showed me that—showed me that I don't have to put up with people taking what they want and giving nothing in return. You can't expect me to forget all that just because you're the one who broke my heart. I can't do it, Will. You have to go now.'

He watched her carefully, taking in the set of her jaw, the clenched fists, the hard eyes. She was right. He'd told her over and over to stand up for what she really wanted. And she'd listened. Part of him was pleased. So proud that she'd finally seen that she was someone who deserved the best from everyone in her life. And another, larger part of him was disgusted, horrified with himself for causing the hurt that was so evident in every part of her body.

He leant against the doorframe, his body drained of energy as he realised he had to go—had to let her go. He didn't want to tempt her or cajole her or try and change her mind. Of all people, *he* knew what it must be costing her to stand her ground. The only thing he could do was leave her now. It wouldn't be right to push his way back into her life.

But a part of him was torn away as he walked back to his car.

Maya sat at the kitchen table, sipping her tea and eyeing the package propped against the fruit bowl suspiciously.

She knew that it was from Will as he'd included a return address on the back. Her pulse had started to race when she'd seen that, and she had felt dizzy as she'd relived that excruciating morning. It looked different to her every time she remembered it. To start with she'd been able to see nothing but his rejection, the way he'd thrown her words of love back at her as if they meant nothing. But as the initial shock had started to wear away she'd seen hurt and nuance and anguish, until she wasn't sure she could be angry for ever.

She'd been staring at the parcel for the best part of half an hour, wondering what more Will could possibly have to say to her. Nothing could undo the hurt he had caused, but the temptation to listen, to try and understand what had gone wrong, was too great. She reached for the envelope taped to the front of the package.

Dear Maya

The book enclosed with this letter is Julia's recipe collection. I hope that you will accept this gift from Neil and me. We were looking through some of her things together, and we both wanted you to have it.

Maya dropped the letter in surprise and reached into the padded envelope. From it she withdrew a hardback notebook, dog-eared and slightly faded with time. She flicked slowly through the pages of neat cursive script, smiling at the evidence of frequent revision: quantities neatly struck through, notes on oven temperatures and timings added in margins. The recipes were diverse, from Christmas cake to meatballs, apple pie to moussaka. They had been added over time, Maya guessed, and captured years of accumulated knowledge and wisdom.

Eventually, after page after page of neat script, she reached one smudged with a sticky handprint and stopped. It couldn't be Julia's hand, Maya knew. The notebook was so neat in every other way. When she glanced at the top of the page she knew instantly who the print belonged to.

Cottage pie. The first meal Will had cooked solo, he had told her, and here was the evidence. The hand was small, she thought, placing hers over it, comparing the size. Nothing like the large, capable hands of the Will she knew. He'd been a child when he'd first cooked that meal, unaware of the loss and the pain that lay before him. Maybe feeling safe and secure and happy for the first time in his life.

Maya swallowed down the lump in her throat and continued reading the letter.

I know that the way I behaved that morning was terrible, and the things I said were unforgivable. You told me you loved me, and instead of telling you that it made my heart swell and ache, that it made me more incredibly lucky than I deserve—which is how I feel now, knowing that you thought it—I lashed out and hurt you.

None of this is an excuse. What I did to you that morning, breaking my promise, is inexcusable. But I want you to know how sorry I am. And that if you ever give me another chance I'll never break a promise, walk away from you, hurt you again.

There's something else I want you to know, and to remember always.

I love you.

Wherever you are, whatever you're doing, saying, thinking, I'll love you.

Will

She refolded the paper and let out a long breath, trying to sort through her thoughts, to make sense of the swirl of her emotions.

He knew her so well—better than she even understood herself. He saw her greatest fears so clearly, and although he couldn't take back what he'd done she knew that she could never be truly alone again, because Will would always love her. She didn't have to try all the time, or even at all. She didn't have to do anything to earn his love. She just had it. Always. He'd never denied that— not even as he was breaking her heart.

But it didn't mean that she could forgive him.

CHAPTER TWELVE

WILL GLANCED AT his phone as he sipped hot, strong coffee. Still nothing. It had been more than a week since he'd sent that letter, since he'd laid himself on the line. And he still hadn't heard a word. He wasn't angry, or even frustrated—he had no right to be; hope had drained away days ago, leaving nothing but a dull, aching pain.

He knew why Maya hadn't answered: he didn't deserve it, didn't deserve *her*. After everything he had said to her, every way he had hurt her, it was impossible that she would forgive him. Even as he'd written the letter he hadn't expected that. But he'd wanted to explain properly. Had to make sure she knew that it was absolutely nothing she had done wrong. That only he was to blame.

Even though he hadn't spoken to her in days he felt Maya's presence all around him, whether he was awake or asleep. She was in every meal and every drink he enjoyed, every caress of soft cotton, even in the warmth of the sun on his face. He felt her presence in everything that brought him pleasure, everything that made him *feel*.

This morning he'd shut his office door, unable to tolerate the looks Rachel was throwing at him every ten minutes: a combination of frustration, pity and 'I told you so'.

At least his work was going well, even if nothing else was. It was the only thing keeping him going, knowing that Julia House was still on track, that he'd not made a mess of everything. But even that was only down to Maya, to the fact that she'd stuck to her word about the fundraiser when she had every reason to change her mind.

Suddenly the shrill bell of his phone shattered the silence of his office, and he knocked over his coffee in his haste to grab it.

Neil.

He pushed down his disappointment as he took the call.

'Hi, Neil. Just give me a minute.' He opened the door and ushered Rachel in to help with his coffee. 'Sorry, I'll have to call you right back.'

He grabbed the napkins Rachel threw at him and blotted the coffee from his keyboard.

'Who was it?' she asked.

'My…my foster dad,' he replied, realising there was no reason he shouldn't say this out loud, no reason to hide his past.

'Oh!' Rachel didn't hide her surprise. 'I didn't… Why don't you call him back from my desk? I'll take care of this.'

'Thanks—he's not been well.'

He sat in Rachel's chair and dialled Neil on his phone, almost unable to believe how simple it was to have Neil back in his life, to reveal this part of himself.

'Neil, sorry about that,' he said with a despondent sigh, leaning forward and resting his forehead in his hand. 'Spilt coffee all over my desk.'

'Let me guess—you thought it was her on the phone.'

He had no idea how this man could still read him like a book after fifteen years, but it brought a small smile to his face, this reminder that the family he'd thought he'd lost wasn't gone for ever. He felt himself relax, just a fraction, felt the darkness lift ever so slightly.

'So she hasn't called?'

'No.'

He leaned back in the chair and watched Rachel mopping up the coffee on his desk, moving the 'Maya Delights' flyer he had propped against his desk-tidy to save it from the flood. He'd told Rachel it was just so he'd have the number handy in case there were any problems about the dinner tonight. She hadn't even bothered to hide her eye-roll.

When he'd returned to his office after a week at Maya's cottage the grey walls had seemed heavy, oppressive. The splash of colour from the flyer made the air seem lighter every time he looked at it.

'And you sent the letter?' Neil said.

'A week ago.'

There was a long silence and Will imagined Neil trying to think of something encouraging to say.

'Well, maybe she wants to do it in person. It's not really the sort of conversation to have on the phone.'

Will shook his head. 'It's not really the sort of conversation to have when we're both working either.' He sighed. Much as he wanted to believe Neil, the weight of Maya's silence was unbearable.

'Maybe she thinks we'll get through the day without talking at all?'

'Are you going to give her that choice?' Neil asked gently.

He took a second to think about it. 'I have to. She knows how I feel. She either wants to try or she doesn't.'

He couldn't keep the defeat from his voice. If she didn't want him he would carry that pain and scar for ever. But he knew that he could never regret meeting her—wouldn't take back having her in his life, not even to spare himself this additional pain.

'You'll definitely be there for the fundraiser?' Will asked.

'Oh, if you're sure? You know these fancy parties aren't really my thing. But if you think it'll help the charity to have me there—'

'It'll help *me* to have you there,' Will admitted, forcing down the lump in his throat.

'Then I'll be there.'

Will grabbed his cufflinks and patted his jacket pockets again. Wallet, keys, phone—exactly where they'd been the last time he'd checked. He fidgeted while he ran through everything he needed to do before he headed to the ballroom. He'd been working for the last hour from the temporary office Rachel had set up at the venue and all seemed to be going well.

Rachel had emailed earlier, telling him everything was in place. She'd made a point of telling him—twice—that the caterers had arrived as planned. His heart-rate had picked up with every mention of Maya's name until he had no longer been able to sit still. He had paced the office for the rest of the afternoon.

Now, standing at the door of the office, waiting to go down, he felt his heart pounding a tattoo in his chest. But he took a deep breath and opened the door, bracing himself.

And walked straight into Rachel.

'I thought you'd be enjoying the champagne by now,' Will said, trying to keep his nerves and frustration out of his voice.

She held up two glasses—one only half full. 'I am. But I thought you might need a little Dutch courage and a push through the door.'

'Thanks.' He grabbed the glass and took a long slug.

'Now through the door.'

'Fine, fine—I'm going.' He went to take another sip of champagne and then stopped himself. Tempting, he thought, but this night would be hard enough even with a clear head.

He headed downstairs, walking rather than taking the lift, delaying the moment when he'd see Maya, look into her eyes, and know she'd read his letter and it hadn't made any difference. He had to brace himself for rock bottom.

As he reached the door of the ballroom his phone buzzed in his pocket. Neil. He was here, thank goodness. It struck him again how much Maya had given him. He had his family back, and he could never repay her for how incredible *that* was. He answered the phone and told Neil he'd see him at the ballroom door.

He stroked his thumb instinctively over his phone, desperate for distraction. But he stopped himself. If a week with Maya had taught him anything it was that fighting off his feelings only made them worse. So instead he focussed on Maya. With her face fixed in his mind, suddenly his body went still: he was centred. Whatever happened, he would see her again tonight. For now, as that was all he could be sure of, it would have to be enough.

Neil finally approached and gave him a slap on the shoulder.

'You ready for this, son?'

'Which bit?' Will asked through gritted teeth, steadying himself with a hand on the wall. 'The fundraiser or Maya?'

'Either. Both.'

He tried to school his features so they didn't show his despair and desperation. 'No.'

'Well, then, that's the spirit,' Neil said with a stoic smile, propelling Will into the ballroom.

Maya stepped back from the kitchen door and held her breath, wondering if he had seen her. She'd spent the entire day with at least half an eye glued to the window in that door, wondering if and when Will was going to turn up. She didn't even know why she was doing it. If she'd wanted to see him she could have done that before now. But she'd woken up that morning with a spark of antici-pation in her chest, and it had grown and grown through the day, pushing against her ribs, forcing out her breath.

Although even if she had wanted to talk to him there'd have been no time. Her wild swings between anger and forgiveness had not helped with her prep, and she was racing the hands of the clock to get everything out on time. And it wasn't over yet. There was still the duck to finish, the plates to dress for the main course, and vegetables to sauté at the last minute.

Difficult enough even *without* the man she loved turning up looking good enough to lick. A rush of love for him hit her like a truck and she felt some of the strength leave her legs, had to lean against the wall. She loved him. She wanted to reach out and touch him. But she couldn't. Because whether she loved him—whether he loved *her*, even—wasn't the question. It was whether she could forgive him, trust him. Whether they had a future together.

She turned it over in her mind time and time again. Would it be risking too much? Asking for her heart to be broken again?

Turning Will away from her house had been only the start of her new life. It was so clear to her now how unbalanced her friendships were—how she'd allowed herself to give everything of herself without ever expecting or even wanting anything in return. And her friendships looked flat, shallow. If she ever wanted them to be anything else the change had to start with her.

So she'd gone to Dylan's birthday party. When Gwen had seen her she had looked a little embarrassed. Stammering out the words, Maya had told her that of course she'd still be happy to watch the children occasionally—as long as Gwen could give her plenty of notice. And perhaps Gwen could help *her* out by watering her herb garden and taking in deliveries when she was in London.

She'd forced the request out, feeling heat and blood rushing to her face, but Gwen had been quick to agree.

They'd both taken a couple of gulps of their wine after that, but the afternoon that followed had been one of the most enjoyable Maya had ever spent outside of a kitchen. Freed from watching her every word, she'd found herself laughing, joking more than she remembered doing before.

But even that step hadn't helped her to see what to do with Will—what to do with her feelings for him. And then the parcel and the letter had shown up: proof of the changes he was making too, proof that the progress he'd made at her cottage that week hadn't been an illusion. And with that knowledge had come the niggling thought that perhaps they could try again.

The knowledge that he loved her had glowed inside her, growing brighter every day, until eventually it had outshone her anger. Because she'd believed him when he said it. After all, he'd never denied it. Not even at his most heartbreaking. He loved her. But a relationship took more than love: it took courage and commitment.

Maya returned to her starters, carefully placing the scallops and finishing the plates with a scattering of herbs, calling for service as she went.

When the last plate was gone she hurried to the door, allowing herself a quick glance across the room. It was a moment before she realised what she was doing, and then another before she found him. He looked up as her eyes reached him and held her gaze across the hustle of the ballroom. She tried to make herself look away, but in his face she saw every touch and every smile they had shared. She remembered how it felt to be in his arms, how he had looked when he'd told her that he loved her.

One of the kitchen porters shouted from behind her and her memories were scattered, replaced by the sizzle of duck breasts crisping behind her. She knew she had to get back to work but she couldn't drag herself away, couldn't break this bond between them. It was still palpable, even with distance, a door and a hundred people between them.

But then he moved to stand, and it broke her trance. *He couldn't come in here.* Her hand flew to her throat at the thought that he might try. Whatever happened, whatever was said, she knew it would leave her drained or high or empty. She needed to focus. She needed *him* to focus. If he couldn't secure the funding he needed tonight then all this would have been for nothing; it would be as if the week at her cottage had never happened. As if *they* had never happened.

She returned to the hotplate with a new sense of purpose. When she glanced up at the window again Will was deep in conversation with the older man sitting next to him. *Good.* She just needed to hold this operation together for another hour or two. Then they would talk.

Maya rubbed the back of her hand over her forehead as the last of the desserts went out and then grabbed a cloth, determined to get the kitchen cleared down in record time. Adrenaline was coursing through her as she knew the time when she would see Will, speak to him, drew nearer.

As she wiped the counters near the door she glanced through the window and saw him heading towards the lectern that had appeared at one end of the ballroom. She hesitated and watched him. His expression was a riot of emotion: nerves, pride, guilt, tension. Watching from across the room, she could still feel the connection that had grown between them at her cottage, the energy that pulled them together, held them there, and she wondered if he felt it too.

She knew that this was hard, whatever it was that he was doing. She could see it clearly in his face and his posture, and she wanted to be here with him. She leaned against the frame and nudged the door open with her foot so she could listen.

Will spoke clearly, thanking everyone there for their support and generosity.

'And now I'd like to say a few words about Julia Wilson and the charity that bears her name,' Will said, with a hint of a waver to his voice.

Her heart ached at the sound of it. Regardless

of what he'd done to her, she loved him, and his pain was her pain.

His hands gripped the lectern tightly as he continued. 'I first met Julia when I was twelve years old. Not long after that first meeting she and her husband, Neil, became my foster parents. They welcomed me into their lives with unrivalled generosity. Julia was generous with her time, her home, her family, her kitchen—'

He gave a small smile and his eyes flickered up. Maya was certain that glance was directed at her.

'And with her love. But when I was fifteen cancer took Julia away from us.'

Will's voice wavered again, and Maya ached to wrap her arms around him, to offer him support and comfort—love. But she stayed where she was. Last time she had offered her help he'd pushed her away and broken her heart.

Will took a long pull on the glass of water in from of him and looked out across the tables before starting to speak again.

'Working with a wonderful board of trustees to make this dinner happen has been rewarding, frustrating and at times very painful. For many years after Julia's death I refused to think about my life with her. It was too painful. But my involvement with the charity has helped me to rediscover happy, joyful memories. It has shown me that the loss of a loved one, no matter how painful, is not the end of everything good. Even in the darkest moments there are people who can offer support and hope, help create good memories along with the bad.

'Before its doors have even opened Julia House has already helped its first patient. If it can help even one more person to find moments of peace and happiness even when—*especially* when—the darkness of their situation seems overwhelming, then I'll be immensely proud of what we've done.'

At these last words he glanced towards the kitchen door, and this time Maya knew that he saw her standing, watching. She wanted to look away, but her gaze refused to drop. She didn't want to lose this moment. The words were for her, she knew, and she felt the connection between them pulse again.

There was nothing more to say.

He had apologised; he had explained. It was down to her now, and no one else, to decide if she could trust him again.

As she saw Rachel striding across the room she pulled her gaze down and backed away from the door, suddenly terrified now that it was time.

'Maya, come on,' Rachel urged, holding open the kitchen door. 'Everyone wants to send their compliments to the chef.'

Maya heard Rachel mumble something about an intervention as she grabbed her hand and dragged her towards the door. She wanted to dig her heels in and sit back on her haunches, to beg to be allowed to hide out in here all night. But she knew that this had to be faced. She was a professional, and this was part of her job. And, even terrified, she wanted to see Will. But her whole life could depend on what happened in the next few minutes.

'Wait,' Maya demanded, reaching for the clip in her hair and running the back of her hand over her forehead. It came away damp with perspiration. 'I'm not going out there like this. I need a couple of minutes.'

Rachel took a step back and folded her arms, a faint smile on her lips. Maya grabbed lipstick, powder and a comb from her bag in the changing room and peered into a mirror.

Applying lipstick under Rachel's scrutiny, Maya

blushed as she realised that she knew everything—
or had guessed.

'Right, I'm ready.'

The other woman reached across and fluffed
her hair a little before leading the way to the door.

The room burst into spontaneous applause as
Maya stepped through the door, and it stopped
her on the spot. The heat in her cheeks grew even
stronger, but her mind was too full of Will to
fully take it in. She glanced around the room and
stilled momentarily. From the kitchen the room
had looked beautiful, but she hadn't truly appreciated the vastness of the space, the opulence of the
fabric draped at the floor-to-ceiling windows. Columns towered around the room, and light danced
from crystal and silver.

A glamorous older woman on the table next to
her reached out to shake her hand.

'Really lovely, dear. I must talk to you about that
sauce for the duck.'

Maya seized the opportunity, grateful that it de-
layed the moment when she would have to decide
once and for all what she wanted.

She made her way from table to table, graciously
accepting compliments, giving hints about her

recipes when people asked, the whole time playing out a weird paradox. She started at the side of
the room furthest away from Will, and the knowledge that he was on the other side of the room
both drew her to him and slowed her progress.
She knew it was inevitable. That she would have
to speak to him at some point. But the closer that
moment got, the more nervous she felt.

She drew out her conversations, always with her
back turned to Will's table, always with him fighting for space in her mind. She tried to force him
out, to focus on anything but him—anything but
the decision she had to make. But finally there
was nowhere else to hide. She took a deep breath,
steadied her shaking hands, and turned to face
Will.

His eyes were already fixed on her, his expression intense and full of love; she stood motionless
as the room and her racing thoughts faded.

'Maya.'

His voice broke the spell and she wanted to
turn and run at the naked tenderness and hope
she heard. She wasn't sure if she could do this,
and nausea crept from her stomach to her throat.

Will stood up as she took a step closer. 'Maya,'

he said again, and then cleared his throat. 'You know Sir Cuthbert and Lady Margery, I think? And this is Neil.'

She nodded at Sir Cuthbert and smiled at his wife. She gaped at Neil, and then reached out and shook his hand, looking from him to Will, marvelling at this repaired relationship. At the courage and forgiveness they must have found to get here.

'It's lovely to meet you, Maya,' Neil said. 'I've heard so much about you from Will.'

She blanched at that. Not *too* much, she hoped.

'Pleased to meet you too,' she said. 'I hope you're well?'

'Yes, never better, thanks. Please—have a seat,' Neil said, pulling a chair over from the next table.

She saw her chance to further delay the inevitable, and engaged Neil in conversation.

'Thank you for the recipe book,' she said, angling her body away from Will. 'It was very thoughtful of you. I hope I can do the recipes justice.'

'I'm sure you will,' Neil said, 'if this evening's anything to go by. The chocolate pudding was incredible.'

She managed a genuine smile at last.

'And I'm glad you like the book. But it was Will's idea. I have to thank you, Maya,' Neil continued, his voice dropping low, 'because I understand from Will that we might still not be in contact if it wasn't for you.'

She shook her head slowly, not sure what she could say to that. Neil and Will had managed to rebuild their relationship, and she was happy for them—truly. But that didn't soothe the pain that had ached in her heart since they day of their reunion.

Suddenly talking to Neil, not talking to Will, was more than she could bear. She knew that she had created the situation by delaying talking to him until they found themselves here, but it didn't matter. She couldn't do it. Not like this. Not yet.

She stood abruptly, the sound of her heart beating loud in her head. 'I hope you all enjoyed the food.' She forced the words out. 'But I really ought to get back to the kitchen. Have a good evening.'

She hurried away from the table, knocking her hip against a chair-back, but kept her eyes fixed forward, refusing to allow herself a glance back.

Her brain was impossibly overloaded. The magnitude of her decision made her head spin, and for a second she thought it was another migraine. At the last minute she realised that the lobby would be a safer exit than the still busy kitchen. She slipped through the door into the foyer and then leaned back against the wall, shutting her eyes and trying to catch her breath.

She just needed a minute to gather her thoughts, to work out what the hell she was going to do about what had happened. When she'd arrived there that morning, she hadn't known what would happen between her and Will. She'd hoped—believed—that at some point the right answer would just come to her, fully formed, and she'd accept it.

She hadn't expected her decision, when she made it, to cause such a tumult of emotion. To leave her so desperate to talk to him, but too afraid to do it. She ran her hands through her hair, trying to calm her thoughts, but her heart was thudding and her palms prickling with stress and tension.

She had learnt so much about Will tonight. He wasn't scared of his memories any more. He wasn't blocking out the good for fear of feeling the bad. The progress that he'd made during the week at her cottage wasn't an illusion. It was real. So how—why?—had he hurt her so badly?

Standing in the lobby, she felt it hit her. She knew exactly why. Because he had felt as over-whelmed and as frightened as she did right now, except he'd had a deadline with life-or-death consequences. He had run because he was confused, exactly as she had just done.

Her eyes snapped open at the sound of a door swinging open.

'Will...' She breathed the word, releasing weeks of anger, longing, loneliness.

He opened his mouth but for a long moment stayed silent. She held her breath.

'Hi.'

They stood together in silence for a few more long, awkward seconds as she tried to think what they could say that would heal this rift between them.

'Can I say something?' Will asked eventually.

Maya nodded nervously, her mouth dry, still not convinced that they could really do this—that they could find one another again.

He took a deep breath and raised a hand to rub at the back of his neck. Maya bit her lip at that en-dearingly familiar gesture.

'If this is going to be the last time I see you,' he

said, rubbing a hand over his eyes now, 'I just want you to know how sorry I am about that morning. It's the biggest mistake I've ever made, and I'll always regret it.'

He looked at her and held her gaze steady for a heartbeat. Two. Then he blinked, looked away. She felt colder without his eyes on her, and his words haunted her. *The last time.* It couldn't be. Her chest felt tight and she knew unequivocally that she couldn't allow that. Knew that she could never forgive herself if she didn't forgive him.

A wave of love for him hit her again as she took in the despair on his face, saw that he expected, wanted nothing from her, that he just wanted to apologise. This was all for *her*, not for him.

'I should go,' he said eventually, his voice flat, empty as he turned, his hand already pushing at the door.

'Will—wait.'

She spoke before she'd had the chance even to think the words. But what more was there to think about? She loved him and he loved her. A relationship took courage and trust. If she didn't step up now, with the first of those, then what chance did they have?

'You hurt me,' she said, and saw his features crumple in pain at the memory of it.

'I know,' he said quietly, his voice full of sorrow. 'And I don't know if I can ever show you how sorry I am, how much I regret it. All I can say is that I love you, and the cost of loving someone never felt as sharp or as terrifying as it did that morning.'

'I know,' she said, reaching out to him and taking his hand. And she did. She understood.

'I would never, ever…' He stopped himself.

'Go on.'

'No,' he said. 'I wanted—needed to apologise in person. But I won't pressure you, try and make you take me back.'

She forced out of rush of breath in frustration, wondering when she was going to get *her* say in this.

'I'm a big girl, Will. And we both know I'm past being forced into anything.'

She thought back to the evening when he'd shown up on her doorstep and she'd stood her ground, and knew that Will had helped her find the strength and confidence to do that.

'I can make my own decisions. So make your case, if you want.'

He hesitated, giving her an astute look.

'If you're badgering I'll stop you.' She couldn't quite believe that the calm, steady words had come from her own mouth.

'I've only got one thing left to say: I love you, and I will never hurt you again. The only thing I want is for you to be happy.'

He turned back to the door, his face set, his shoulders stiff, and had one foot through it when Maya cleared her throat. He looked back at her, and for the first time she saw a suggestion of hope in his eyes.

'And do *I* get a say?' she asked, one brow raised, her shoulders relaxing as she planted her hands on her hips. 'Because I'm pretty sure someone spent a lot of time recently telling me how important it is that I get what *I* want. I get to decide what makes *me* happy.'

She took a couple of steps towards him and reached for his hand again.

'I want *you*,' she said, looking him straight in the eye. 'You freaked out and got scared and messed up. And don't worry, because I'm already thinking of a thousand ways you can start making that up to me.' She smiled. 'But I heard the speech you gave in there. I saw you with Neil. And I know how it feels when you know what you need to do and you're absolutely terrified of it at the same time. I know you're scared too, but you're trying. And I think I can do that too.'

'Maya…'

He still looked pained, but she wanted him to see that he didn't need to be, that they could overcome this, could be happy—both of them.

'No, Will. You want me to make decisions for *me*? Well, this is my decision, and I'm choosing to give us a chance.' She took another step forward, closing the space between them, and then reached up and cupped his cheek with her palm. 'You told me I should start asking for what I want, what I need. I need *you*: are you going to argue with me?'

She stretched up on tiptoes and brought her lips to Will's. He kissed her back, tentatively at first, as if he couldn't quite believe it. And then hungrily, with his arms wrapping tight around her waist, lifting her practically off her feet, pressing her into the wall behind her.

His hand moved from her waist to tangle in her hair, winding tightly, holding her close. Her nerve-endings felt as if they were burning, and every touch of his hands, his lips, his chest, raised another fire. But she sensed desperation in the wild passion of Will's kiss, and it made her sad.

She eased her lips away from his a fraction and looked up, caught his eye.

'Will, maybe…'

'Too much? I just can't quite believe you're giving me another chance. I never want to let go of you again.'

She stroked her fingertips across his cheek, soothing him, and stopped his words with a quick, gentle kiss. 'It was…well, incredible…'

For a second she forgot why she'd stopped him, and was leaning in to him again when she remembered.

'I'm not going anywhere.' She moved her hand back to his cheek and pushed him away from her, made sure he was looking her in the eye. 'It doesn't matter if you grab me tight, or kiss me gently, or if you just throw me a glance from across the room. I'm yours. I love you and I'm going nowhere. Ever.'

Will closed his eyes and leant his forehead against hers, and for the first time that day she sensed a stillness, a peace about him.

'I love you,' he breathed.

She smiled and closed her eyes, absorbing the truth and power of his words.

'So what now?'

What a question, she thought, thinking of the years, the decades of their life ahead of them. And suddenly she knew with startling clarity what she wanted for that life. Simply him. For ever. A smile curled the corner of her lips as the answer formed in her mind, and then nerves fluttered in her belly as she tried to give it voice.

She lifted her head, the smile beaming from her now. 'Marry me.'

Will dropped his hands from her hair, but her smile never faltered. How could it when she trusted his love for her? When she had so much faith in him? She knew she just had to wait, give him a chance to catch up with her.

Then his face broke into a grin. 'Isn't that my line?'

'Nope. It's what I want, so I'm the one who asks for it.'

'You're incredible,' Will said, dipping his head for a kiss.

Maya stopped him with a palm against his chest. 'Are you going to answer?'

'Yes,' Will said with a chuckle. 'Always, always yes.'

Maya curled her hand around his shirt and pulled him to her, meeting his lips with her own.

* * * * *

Maya stopped him with a palm against his chest. 'Are you going to answer?'

'Yes,' Will said with a chuckle. 'Always, always yes.'

Maya curled her hand around his shirt and pulled him to her, meeting his lips with her own.

* * * * *

'I love you,' he breathed.

She smiled and closed her eyes, absorbing the truth and power of his words.

'So what now?'

What a question, she thought, thinking of the years, the decades of their life ahead of them. And suddenly she knew with startling clarity what she wanted for that life. Simply him. For ever. A smile curled the corner of her lips as the answer formed in her mind, and then nerves fluttered in her belly as she tried to give it voice.

She lifted her head, the smile beaming from her now. 'Marry me.'

Will dropped his hands from her hair, but her smile never faltered. How could it when she trusted his love for her? When she had so much faith in him? She knew she just had to wait, give him a chance to catch up with her.

Then his face broke into a grin. 'Isn't that my line?'

'Nope. It's what I want, so I'm the one who asks for it.'

'You're incredible,' Will said, dipping his head for a kiss.